I0822718

Of Circumstances and Intrigues

Joseph Warren Morris

New Branch
PUBLISHING

New Branch Publishing
7454 Huntwick Trail
Nashville, TN 3722
Email: newbranchpublishing@gmail.com
Phone: 615-646-0755

Of Circumstances and Intrigues

First published by New Branch Publishing

ISBN 978-0-9988528-0-5

This book is printed on acid-free paper.

Graphics by Jera Publishing

Printed by Lightning Source

Printed in the United States of America
Nashville, Tennessee

Previous Books by Joseph W. Morris

Little Valley of Germania

Cowboy

The Atonement of Sasha

Of Circumstances and Intrigues

About the Author

Joseph W. Morris, a native Tennessean, was educated in Texas, Tennessee, and Mississippi; he attained the Ph.D at the University of Mississippi.

A good many of his most poignant experiences were singularly associated with his farm life in the South, where as a lad he picked the cotton and sang the songs that old Negro field hands picked and sang, toiling with them side by side, there increasingly sensitized to their mode of culture.

His range in terms of depth and substance springs in part from his adventures in the western sector of the nation, this starting when he went off to Texas for college, soon, in need of money, wandering into the oil fields seeking part time employment and finding it on the oil slick drilling rig platforms of North Texas: and upon graduation left for the vast fruit growing region of the San Joaquin and Sacramento Valleys of California where the crops were planted and harvested by scores of ethnics, then by and large Mexican, Japanese, and Philippine. Here he was hired as a management trainee by one of the nation's largest soup producing corporations. Within a short while he left for the University of Mississippi where he met up with the renowned William Faulkner.

Acknowledgement

I cannot offer praise enough to Jera Publishing for their services to me in the preparation and publication of this work. They are admirable in the execution of their art, among the very best in the broad field of literature productions. I am fortunate to have acquired their assistance in this and previous endeavors.

Preface

Once the author, my friend, revealed to me that Hemingway, at one time or another, expressed that he had never gotten around to writing a novel, that he had sunk into a fixity, the trait of concentrating only on the short story. But my friend was gladdened that the great writer reversed himself and produced two immemorial works for the world to absorb and enjoy, *Farewell to Arms* and *For Whom the Bell Tolls*. It was but a brief while thereafter that he himself said that his experience seemed to run to the opposite of Hemingway's previous choices, that his devotion to the novel had been his unaltered bent and that his adventure with the short story came to him through virtual chance. It so happened that upon the near halfway mark of a rather lengthy undertaking, another novel, he discovered in one of his previously finished chapters, indeed a short story. "There it was, suddenly, my first, "The Killing," he said, which appears at the front in this series of eight. It sprang to him through this singular experience that there dwelled in his latent internal self an untapped penchant for conceptualizing and weaving together a litany of events and images that could be told ever so briefly and vowed always to continue the pursuit of this medium. And soon seven others followed.

It should be stressed that all eight are unalike in terms of tone and substance and plot but more than that. I have avidly read these works and find in addition to what I have just said that they more than contain the ingredients which all stories must possess to be provocatively rare. They are, in other words, replete with incidents of brutality, of desperation, of tragedy, of bravery and fear, of humor, of uplifting spirit, of conflict and reconciliation, of love gone wrong and love gone right, all this and more. *Of Circumstances and Intrigues* is an enormously fine piece of work and well worth your reading.

Anonymous

Contents

The Killing

I DEARLY LOVED my literature teacher's lectures, but even beyond that, his required readings, broad and deep and rich, extending from the treatises of the ancient Pericles to tales of American romances improvised by Hawthorne and those of a more rugged and torrid substance created both by Faulkner and Hemingway in their works of the modern period. But he did more, handing out assignments to each of us to try our hand and our minds at creating original short stories.

"What kind of stories?" one student spoke out, and I was glad for his effort because it saved me from having to ask the same.

"Choose. You choose what you wish young man. It's your choice. That's part of being creative. But keep it to less than three pages. I don't hear as good as I once did," this last line thrown in as intended humor.

The first student to finish with her creation, which happened on the third day from the assignment, was asked to read it aloud and the title dawned upon me as a profoundly well contrived piece of work, *A Replica of my Home Town,* a suave erudite selection to my way of thinking, the content superiorly written and Dr. Linskie felt as much too, but in so many words said also that the content came across a bit stilted, simply made up from scratch, and that the best stories evolved from the convolutions of real life. It apparently seemed to him that the town of which she spoke did not exist, that it had been fantasized. But appraised the whole of her creation generously in his summary. At the end of the session he turned to me with the casual remark that he would expect me to deliver my story when the class again assembled. Afterwards I held back and just before he left the room I asked if I might also write about my home town and that I was toying with the idea and had done so for two days and that it involved a tragedy.

"In your home town?"

"Yes sir."

"It's fresh upon you then, so proceed. I'll look forward to hearing of it."

And so when the class next met Dr. Linskie merely signaled to me to station myself at the head of the room and begin.

"My story is real. It lingers firmly entrenched in my recall to this day, and also sadly to this day. It involves a killing when I was a little boy, too young to comprehend the meaning of the term or why a killing took place. I did not witness the act, nor did I hear people speak of it until I was some years older when my father let me go into town with him. It was a Saturday afternoon, people crowded together on the street side in front of the several serried stores. My mother sat at my father's side in the front seat of the wagon. 'Look,' he said to her lowly, 'there's Albert Roberts, he's out of the penitentiary.' She replied with a tinge of animation, if not anxiety in her voice, 'Yes, I see him. Why is he out?'

'I guess he's done his time, enough anyway I'm taking it for them to let him loose.'

I saw the man about whom they were talking, Albert Roberts, short, stocky, red faced, a slight hunch at the shoulders, graying, overweight at the midriff, and wearing a straw hat. While leaning against one of the rounded steel posts that upheld the canopy of the store front he conversed with someone as ordinarily as any other citizen. That night after supper I asked my father what was killing, the thing I'd heard them speak of during the day, the reply coming, done as carefully and patiently as he knew how, that it was the taking of another's life; and after this had sunk in I naturally began to pursue him further, my mother on pins and needles because she feared that such graphicness might be harmful to the emotions of her young son. But it was too late. 'How did it happen? Why did Mr. Roberts kill another man?'

'I don't think he truly meant to son. I don't. He was kind of put up to it. Egged on by some of the meddlers who liked to get into other's business. The fracas started when Albert and another man got into an argument. They were hot, shouting at one another while out on the street with a crowd bunched around gawking, itching to see a fight. Luckily, the constable, who was summoned from some place in town, stepped in and separated them before blows were landed, and it seemed that the last of the confrontation had worked up to a head and then and there got settled for good.

The other man left, they said, going to Meadeville, in his wagon five miles away, telling someone before he left that he'd try to make it back before sundown. In the meantime there were some — the instigators — who got into Albert's ears that he had been insulted, made light of, had lost the argument, and that to save his honor he should intercept the man on his way from Meadeville and even the score. I think Albert tried to resist. They said he did. But the words from the instigators kept pouring into his head and didn't slow down. More and more words just kept coming. Suddenly something snapped inside. He wheeled and lit out for the livery stable across the railroad track and at no slow pace, hitched up his team, and set out toward Meadeville. Who knows what happened after that except that at the trial Albert confessed under relentless pressure from the prosecuting attorney that he went as far as the river bottom, half way between here and Meadeville, unhitched his horses and hid out of sight until the hated image of the man he quarreled with drew abreast, and there he shot him with a sawed off double barrel shotgun at close range.

I think my mouth stayed half open during the entire telling. It was almost too much. As I grew older I realized that sooner or later, everyone, every child, must hear of such tragedies, an inevitable part of living I judged, and that my father viewed that one time was as good as another for me to learn of Albert Roberts and the hideous crime he committed. Eventually, I adjusted to the fact that an assailant lived among us in our small town, yet as I came to know and be around him, though reservedly, I found him friendly, likeable, and kind natured, and it seemed almost unthinkable that in his breast he nurtured the capability, or once nurtured it, of slaying another. Making this more unfathomable were his two daughters, Ruth and Annie, lovely young women, Ruth in time joining the church that I attended and settling in as an avid member of my mother's Sunday school class. Annie, the more gorgeous of the two girls, started to work in Memphis at the Sears store and every Friday evening at seven o'clock during the summer I saw her getting off the greyhound bus, in route to her parent's home for the weekend.

I will continue to think of those girls over the coming years as the years approach one by one, and for me this is pretty much the end of my story, but for them there is no end. As a relentless curse they'll carry the stigma with them on and on no matter where they go or live. After a lapse of years other attentions will slowly fill up the local people's minds, letting the incident fade into mist, but not so of the family who lived through it all, the older ones especially. It will to them forever remain indelible. The young, family and non family born years later, will know little of it and whatever they might know, if anything at all, will in their revolving amount to no more than an unseemly tale of the past. In my own instance I have tried to forget it. I'd like to. But there remains one glaring reminder that won't let me, for when I go back from time to time to pay respects to my kindred who reside in the Mount Pisgah Cemetery, where my father and mother will lie, my path leads me to the tombstone which reads, 'Here lies Albert and Lavada Roberts.' That is all I will see, no other epithet; nothing of his reputation or the foulness of his crime, and that is as it should be."

Upon finishing, I ambled toward my chair, with an aim to sit promptly down, but was instantaneously distracted by a rising tumult, an applause from my classmates, I discovered as I glanced about, who did not hold back with their congratulations of acclaim. Doctor Linskie applauded as well, an obvious approval appearing in his aging smiling face. I had succeeded and I knew why. It was the story, not me, that ignited them, a simple story with a singular theme which consisted of the exact necessary characteristics. I was not surprised, recalling one of the gratuities of advice that my dear professor shared with me when I took one of his lower level classes: "If you write Ramsey, and you really want to mesmerize your readers, write of tragedy. Draw out the dark side of humanity and the pain that comes with it even though it may go against your natural taste. Innately people are endowed of a liking to be stunned by the description of a terrifying scene in which great inescapable harm to someone or to several has come to bear. Poe capitalized on this technique and it paid off; he earned a living from it, and I have avidly read his works, all of them over and over. He was a genius at story telling, albeit in my opinion a slight nipped in the head. But that is another matter, is it not?"

The Mayor and the Young Reporter

IT WAS a dance. The Mayor's dance the city folks said, those in high circles, a Ball in actuality and the young girl Lenora envisioned it with mixed emotions, on the one hand elated at the idea of attending the affair and yet on the other, wishing to avoid going.

"The Mayor's Ball, hmmmm, put together by the Womens'League. Makes me nervous."

It was her first event ever like this, an unsettling thought to a rural girl fresh out of high school ungroomed as yet in the suave customs of upper society. She wished again she could discover a way out but none came to her — none that she felt believable or acceptable to her boss, the editor of a well known newspaper in a well known city of the South who had asked her to cover the extravaganza.

"So I can't back out; it's an assignment, part of my job. I'm a green junior reporter, and this is my first big chance. No, no backing out. I'm going." But she paused as if suddenly in ponder. "Let me think. I'll need someone with me. Certainly. I'll ask Charles, that new reporter just like me, if he'll consent to being my escort. He hired in along with me, on the very same day."

She would ask him at lunch, where the reporters congregated in mass to eat, and at lunch she asked, having enticed him to a corner recluse equipped with a table for not more than two where she could talk to him alone.

"What! Me!" Was it so that this enchanting girl of captivating natural charm — at whom every male in the department uncontrollably gawked when she passed through — now spoke to him of attending the Mayor's Ball and that she would be delighted to have him accompany her?

Upon sufficient recovery he stammered yes and then more distinctly when she asked him to enunciate it again because he seemed incomprehensibly blurry about what he had said. "If you mean it Lenora. Yes, I'll gladly go with you. When is it?"

"In two weeks, on a Thursday evening."

As time neared she began to finalize her attire, deciding on a simple gown, nothing extraordinaire, nothing to match the standards of the rich socialites with their expensive wardrobes and exquisite tastes and glittering bracelets and necklaces. But she, as was so of all women of that era, wished for a pair of silk hose rather than those fabricated from synthetic nylon, which by and large women in general regarded as an inferior substitute. But she would not fret, for even the upper ladies were not spared of the disappointment. The fifty-one gauge nylons would have to do, for after all, parachutes were vital to the war effort, the war against the Germans and Japanese, and since parachutes were comprised of silk no woman dared think of the use of this precious material for hosiery.

The day came, the young escort rang the door bell, now aglow and walking on clouds at having the honor of the most beautiful girl in the whole city clinging to his arm as they made their way among the throng of eloquent people attired in lovely colorful shimmering gowns and dark tuxedos. Suddenly she appeared as the door opened. His heart raced. Never had he seen her like this nor could he ever have called it into his imagination. On her slim envied figure the attire of an emerald green evening gown with a scooped neck hung eloquently, but with exact properness —this gorgeous piece paid for from months of personal savings at a part time job back home. There was as well a simple pearl necklace that wound jealously in three strands around her long firm neck; and her hair, dark and shiny, fell in soft waves upon creamy white shoulders. A cab waited; so they went and climbed in, Charles helping her, opening and closing the door, and in no lengthy time were there. Upon leaving their transport and going but a few paces to the frontage they were admitted by the doorman. A distinguished couple stood at another doorway further inside the foyer, assigned to the purpose of speaking nice affable welcomes to incoming guests and upon instant sight recognized Lenora and Charles from an earlier description supplied by an official at the newspaper.

"Good evening Miss Somers; Good evening Mr. LaGrange. We're glad to see you and are most happy that you decided to come." It fell strangely on Lenora that anyone could be addressing her by the honorific, Miss, and struggled a bit to remember a time when anyone did that unless in her mid grades where the teachers were teaching the young girls the art of finery in greeting and being greeted. Having thought as much she graciously returned that she and Charles were delighted to attend and warmly appreciated that the hosts were acting as if they knew them almost personally. Then they turned and left, the lady glancing at Lenora repeatedly, her admiration keenly following as long as they stayed in sight.

Entering the hallway just off the expansive Ballroom they delayed. Both nervous. measuring. "Well, here goes," said Lenora, softly, administering a hardly discernible squeeze to Charles's arm. Mustering courage and taking a breath they entered the Ballroom mezzanine and found themselves at the top of the steps leading to the grand dance floor below, now bulging with happy chatting people, rich people talking rich people talk, and filled with lovely refrains wafting from the violins. The orchestra played a waltz as they descended the steps and were led to their tables. The young man at her side basked proudly and fashioned a smile as if to say to anyone watching, "she's mine." Her persona waxed warm and sparkling, a God given quality and as they passed along heads turned and questioning glances shot forth in abundance. As they were seated whispers began to sweep throughout the room. "Who's that?" an envious voice arose, or perhaps the voice sounded of a view of pure admiration, for many were those that admired. How could they not? At any event introductions were exchanged with others at their table and the evening got underway. Lenora and Charles danced the very next dance together. By any measure he could not be classed as a good dancer, not a shortcoming however that she dared mention, but she herself danced exceedingly well, a near virtuoso, and easily and gracefully covered his lacking, thanks to the lessons she took under the scrutinizing eye of her ballroom high school teacher. Some young man with the air of a courtesan whom she had met before though not remembering where or when asked her if he might have the next dance. She accepted. She had to. The societal rules of this grand affair considered it inappropriate conduct for a young lady to decline a young man's request and to have done as much would have reflected poor breeding and undeserving status. She could not see it coming but her acceptance opened the gates to a flood of requests which kept her busy until Charles managed to rescue her, taking her back to their table. For awhile they sat and looked on.

"Is the Mayor here?"

"Why? Are you going to dance with him?"

"I didn't say that. Just wondering if he were here."

"He's here and I have to add that he seems to enjoy watching you dance. He must. Every time I glance over he has you in his sights."

"You're kidding. Why would he look at me?"

"Hmm. Probably because you're the most beautiful girl here, or it could be he's read your editorials and seen your photographs."

"Do you suppose he's angry because of the editorials, taking it I'm singling him out personally?"

"I can't say. But I think you're likely to find out pretty quickly. He's coming our way along about now."

She sighed. "Goodness!"

Sure enough the Mayor edged through the crowd towards the table where they sat, though as he came nearer someone tugged at his sleeve, a gentleman wanting a word with him and it appeared in Lenora's thoughts that his attention could not be trained on them, the most unlikely of things, and that as soon as he left the gentleman who presently engaged him he might by some quirk choose to pass close to them while on his way to converse with a dignitary of political importance. But that he would come no closer. Yet, hardly a flicker had expired when the Mayor bid his acquaintance good evening and resumed his original course, there being no doubt of his intentions. Lenora looked down at her hands resting limp on the table.

"My Goodness! It's on the verge of happening. It really is. But wait. Why am I so timid about this? It's not like me. I have a stiffer spine. I will not shrink from his presence. If it's me the Mayor is seeking I will meet him head on, and proudly, as my parents have always taught me to do in situations of test."

Suddenly there were a pair of black patent leather shoes at rest near her chair, and as she turned, her courageous lovely face inclining hesitantly upward, there he was, Boss Crump, the Mayor, smiling warmly downward at her.

"Good evening Miss Somers," he said with a slow Southern dialect of a sonorous intonation, a voice of sureness and confidence as is so of personages of power in high office. "The next dance is a waltz and it would be my exceeding pleasure if you consented to share it with me. Will you?"

She had prepared herself, answering with poised civility and charm, a living trace of the societies of Antebellum, a lingering remnant of the customs and courtesies practiced by kindred generations of that era and for awhile afterwards. Her finesse at public mingling by this stage had reached a near peak of delicately cultivated sophistication; much of it owed to her best friend, her mother, who had been both teacher and prompter.

"Mr. Crump, thank you. The pleasure is mine."

She arose from her chair, Charles frantically scooting it back for her, and extended her hand of acceptance, the Mayor taking it and cradling it in his as if it were a toy that might break unless treated with infinite care, and then they walked together to the dance floor and began to dance. The orchestra had struck the first chord already. Lenora beamed in elated silence. "If the people back home could see me now!"

"Miss Somers, you are an excellent dancer and a very lovely one at that," the Mayor said before they had gone less than half the circumference of the room. Her heart pounded so that she was sure he felt it, which wasn't possible because they danced with arms extended as was the custom that evening. "It's my imagination playing tricks on me," she quickly decided. "I'll have to get a better grip on myself," and she would but her undaunted bravery for the moment had subsided to an uncustomary low. .

"Oh Mr. Mayor, you're kind. And I wish I could say more to express my appreciation for your praise which in all fairness I don't deserve. But you see. Well, it doesn't show I guess but I'm afraid I'm a little nervous. Not much but some. I'm not really accustomed to attending gala affairs like this."

"Ah! I can't believe what you say. Miss Somers, you show no nervousness, not in the least. If you are you're a magician at hiding it. And insofar as your being unaccustomed to gala affairs is concerned let me say this: if I didn't know better I'd swear you've gone to no telling how many in your young lifetime. I'll even go further. And I mean it down to the bottom of my shoes. You're the Belle of this Ball this evening. The Belle of this Ball. Take it from me you are. No one else is even close." Not remotely suspecting these stunningly glowing compliments she could retrieve no words for what she thought would be a suitable response and so instead continued to smile and look compellingly up into his face. He would say more but to himself. "What a refreshing contrast to, to, to those over attired ladies as usual; just look at her, so sweet, so shy, a beauty. I like her honesty, her innocence, and obviously she is of remarkable intelligence. I know that. I keep abreast of her every editorial which appears in the morning paper, never missing a one."

"How did you get interested in politics Lenora?"

"Lenora! He called my name. It's like he knows me." The countenance of her expression evinced that she at once experienced a surge of delight at his personalization but wondered how he had come to know her first name. It took but a tad. "The editorials girl. It's the editorials. Don't you get it?"

"I've always been keenly taken with how government works. Politics if you will. And as far back as I can remember my ultimate ambition was to be a journalist. You know sir better than anyone else I'm sure that journalism and politics are in a way inseparably knotted. I also like history and it too kind of fits into the picture. Then, let me not leave out, my editorial boss at the paper expects me from time to time to cover political events and is out of his way attentive to groom and meticulously counsel me so that I will always remain neutral and not get ignorantly drawn in."

Even while she talked she told herself that she spoke too much, but the Mayor seemed to be hungrily drinking in every word.

He laughed loudly. It was his habit to laugh loudly. "That answers my question. And based on what I see in your work you're doing everything absolutely right."

As the music played they danced on and her mind began to see the Mayor in still a different perspective, in a light that had not uncloaked itself to her as vividly as now. She read his soul, a self finished, self educated man from the alluvial fertile soils of Mississippi, an adventuresome sort who had run the gauntlet of politics since early age, clawing his way up, not only surviving but flourishing — who possessed a well spring of kindness and generosity in his heart and freely spread these sentiments to those with whom he became enamored.

"He's the Boss, as they all call him, the Mayor of a big city. An important person, but he's human too. I can see that he is. A really nice man. Some things I've heard said of him make him seem awesome. But he really is a nice man; and there's a funny side to him too." She smiled to herself as she recalled and sorted through the more humorous stories she had come across.

"A penny for your thoughts Lenora."

Suddenly. Emerging from her reverie. "Oh! For a moment I got caught up in the music and glamorous people dancing around us." Then she unveiled the truth. "But it didn't concern those things. Not really. It was about you."

"Me! Oh! Tell me."

"If you don't think you'll mind," she said, a trickle of shyness leaking through.

"I promise faithfully."

"Mister Mayor, I've heard and read so many things about you. I'm just wondering if they're all true."

At first the temptation to laugh tried hard to break through but he discovered that it lacked the strength of completion, for the question was sincerely delivered with an irresistible cuteness and innocence that blocked his urge to laugh even before it left his chest. He could but grin.

"Which ones are of especial interest to you?"

She hesitated, not feeling able to judge how much further to go.

"I'm from a very small town Mr. Mayor and some of the things you've done, as I've discovered in researching your background, make me think you're a country boy at heart."

This time he laughed, loudly, uproariously. And said in silent exclamation, "Isn't that hilarious? Country boy. She calls me a country boy. I'll have to tell my wife about that this very night when I get home."

"I am. I am. I proudly am."

"And I sir am a country girl."

"You are? I'll be hanged. I never would have guessed it."

"But I am sir."

"Where from?"

"Yazoo City."

"I'll be hanged again. Not far from where I was born and raised. Small world."

"Indeed."

"How come you got off up here to Memphis?"

"To work."

"I see. Well, you said there are other things as concerns me. For instance? "

"Let me think. Oh yes! Do you really like to walk barefoot over at the horseshoe hunting club after a rainfall like they say you do, with the mud oozing up through your toes?"

And then he roared again. "I love every minute of it Lenora. Every minute of it."

"What an adorable girl," he mused. "So clever at working her will and disarming you without even trying. What an asset she would be to my staff."

They had danced well beyond his intention at the beginning, not more than two rounds which lapsed into not three, not four, but five, or the middle of, which now was the present, wherein he said as chivalrously and as charmingly as his unschooled convention of etiquette would let, "What! We have gone into the fifth round, much longer than I should have kept you. Forgive me. But I am glad. You have turned my evening not only into something enjoyable but also beautiful. I cannot thank you enough."

"Mr. Crump you are more than nice to say these very flattering things to me. You have been the highlight of my evening. I'll never forget it."

As they began to move toward her table he reflected in the little time left on an idea which he had previously entertained, though deciding against relaying it to her. He deemed it hasty at the time. Now he had changed his mind. "When we were dancing Lenora it occurred to me that we could use a person like you on my staff, and, and, before you decline let me finish. I know you are young and I'm sure you are fond of your job, but things can change. So I just want to say this and nothing more. If it happens that you wish to explore something new, please call me personally."

"Oh sir. Thank you. Thank you very much."

The dance having ended the Mayor escorted her to her table, there turning her over to Charles.

"Here you are young man" he drawled, as he gave her hand to him and said teasingly, "lucky young man," then bowed with distinctive courtesy and began to pick his way slowly back to rejoin his party of associates and friends.

Charles overflowed with curiosity. "What did you and the Mayor so busily discuss in all that time you were out there?"

"Not so fast Charles. Give me a chance to recover. Besides, I'm not sure I can remember," and at this he hugged her while to his amazement she rested her face against his shoulder, but then, realizing that people were watching — canvassing her every propriety, no matter how trivial — she sat suddenly erect and looked over at her companion with an impish playful grin. "But even if I do you won't believe a word of what I tell you."

The Skaters

KNOWING EYES did not dwell attentively on the skaters going effortlessly through their configurations as required by the rules of the contest, looking instead at him, and thought his thoughts — of who he had been, of who he now was, and of what lay smoldering in his heart. Not once but often, who could count the times, he claimed the prize himself in his heyday, once in this same arena, his partner too, a graceful lovely Russian girl whose hand he had won and taken for his wife, but whom he later divorced and after this, after years of delay, married another, Emanuelle, now an integral part of the pair he sat watching, stolidly, intently, as if a sphinx. The knowing eyes looked at the skaters, and then again at him, gathering that he saw not the slightest trifle in their artistry that necessitated correction, and this was so because in their performance no one could find the slightest of fault, not even him. From the first Sergi Zakarov had been their coach, a renowned personage of past Olympic fame, and she, his young beautiful wife and pupil — and partner to the tall handsome serene young man at her side, who with her, like gracious floating swans, skimmed across the gray placid ice as once he did. Sergi Zakarov was in years twice the age of his wife, a fact well known and talked of, and it was observed that he had added poundage to his loins and mid riff and that alarmingly, thin streaks of gray had begun to course through his once attractive head of bulky dark hair. Otherwise he had everything. In his possession there were two virtuosos who had won time and again against formidable competition and unless some unforeseen infringement cropped up that blocked their way they would go on winning. What man of that creative yen would have failed to caress from his inner most depth the form and shape of his beautiful skaters, who without his grasp and perseverance would in all probability have fallen shy of their lofty climb and possibly not made it at all. But such exhilaration that should have outwardly showed itself did not appear anywhere in Sergi Zakarov's face, a face cold and mask like, expressionless, and gave no notice, not once, to the tumultuous roar of the spectators who applauded his pair for a difficult maneuver they had just exacted.

Round and round they flew and soared, the eyes down to the last spectator weighing fascinatingly upon them, the eyes of the judges likewise, and all confident that the winners of that evening were those two that darted here and there with amazing acrobatics in this famous arena because they were winners there so often before, no one able to remember when they lost a competition except when they were fledgling beginners. Even to the unknowledgeable it seemed their executions came with the greatest of ease, magnificently done, their footwork together flawless, the girl's pirouettes a thing of beauty, their every turn, every curl, synchronized perfectly with the music, deep and masculine — Russian music — thus reflecting the vastness, the culture, and the strength of that great domain.

So round and round they continued, until upon completion of one final pattern, their performance over, they came front and center to stand side by side, while the crowd more than pleased generously applauded. But something seemed amiss. The French couple who preceded them bubbled over with a real or feigned affection for one another so extreme that they were seen as one, comments sometimes in stretched description going so far as to suggest that it could not be easily determined where one began and the other ended. But that would amount to too much. It came with little effort to see however that they appeared to be irretrievably in love, and of easy consequence to believe they were. They could only be viewed in that light. Not so of Sergi Zakarov's pair, who stood emotionless. To be sure every viewer in that grand facility knew they had won, yet where were the smiles, and more singularly the smiles at one another, and the embraces, and the quickened happy glances that were so apparent in the faces and mannerisms of the French? Strangely, they seemed as automatons; existing without soul.

When the roar of the crowd subsided they bowed in acknowledgement and glided across the way to where the husband coach sat, where, when reaching his whereabouts the young beautiful girl paused and kissed his cheek, then proceeded to take her place by her partner to await the judges' score. A perfect mark.

So close they sat, so beautiful and young, but ah, their proximity, their daily presence with each other hour after hour! What fateful promise. There trickled a moment when she started to smile into his eyes and to touch his arm but slightly, melting sentiments that tempted a return, but he held back. Incisive eyes from the stands did not let it go unnoticed; they clearly saw. Fire smoldered in their hearts, though well contained by both, afraid to let it out lest it burst into open flame; and the husband saw it too, many times he had, afraid of what it meant, desperately holding on, without weapons to fight the battle that his best reasoning told him he would surely lose.

The meets continued for awhile. Once Sergi Zakarov missed, wasn't there, the officials wondering why and when the next meet neared the report surfaced that neither he nor the skaters would be there to participate and with the receipt of this news the officials were flabbergasted, hastening to send word of inquiry, which revealed that illness incapacitated one of the skaters, though not specifying who. They were gladdened when told that the illness should be taken as temporary and that soon the skaters and their coach were to return. Yet, upon receipt of subsequent news they realized that the first of the absences signaled the beginning of the end for the coach and his wonderful skaters, that something uncorrectable stirred within this oddity and that as far as they were concerned, as sad as it was, they must strike them from the venue and begin to look for replacements.

The girl no longer lived with her husband on the nearby sea coast of the Adriatic, at some recent point moving in with her mother who lived alone in Tirana, the capitol city of Albania. She no longer skated, but saw her former partner with unvarying regularity, very much in love with him and he with her she told her mother, who when a girl herself married a man fifteen years her senior, Emanuelle's father.

"And you are taken with this young man whose name is, is, is Alexi Konstanty you say." His name did not live readily on her finger tips. Skating did not interest her; she had never attended a professional meet, and paid but vague attention to the various names of her daughter's acquaintances when they were mentioned.

"I am Momma. He is in my heart."

"Ha. In your heart. Could it be something else?"

"What do you mean?"

"I mean that you are perhaps confused. Mixed up."

"I'm in love with him and he is with me."

"Then perhaps both of you are mixed up."

"Why do you say that Momma? You hurt me. You should be more understanding."

"Bah! Do not even think that, much less speak it. Listen to me. Sergi Zakarov is a good man, a caring man, who's gone through a lot, and much of it because of you."

"You don't know him. You've seen him only at church. His feet have not once crossed the threshold of this home. How can you know he's done so much?"

"I have heard. In addition to molding you into a star he has gone overboard to be kind to you, to see after your every need and if his treatment of my daughter had worked to the contrary I would have known. I have friends. They have kept me informed."

"Well."

"Don't say well. Better that you listen. You want to leave Sergi Zakarov because of this young fawn you call your Alexi, your skating partner, who has tantalized you. How tempting it is for young women to let the wine of passion flow to their head."

"You're unfair."

"No my darling. Just truthful and sensible. I love you and want for you the best of life, so listen to me, to the story that I will now tell. Your once living father exceeded me by fifteen years when I married him. He loved me, he cared for me. Once I took sick, badly bed ridden, and he attended me as well as any superiorly trained nurse; he was my nurse, my everything, cooking, laundering clothing, seeing that I took my medicine, holding me when I ached, and sometimes sat up with me the whole night through pressing an ice pack to my head. The flu epidemic raged as a fire throughout our community. Many died. What would I have done without him? I would have died too, that's what. But I did not die. I lived, saved by your father, an older man who helped me cling to life, and a little later I gave birth to you. To be sure there were chances arising now and then. I was young and pretty and knew it, and saw others look at me, and drool. I could have picked who I wanted. But no. I wasn't a fool. I dashed the temptation from my thoughts and never let it in again, never."

"But I am not you and the circumstances are different."

"How?"

"My husband Sergi Zakarov is getting old, and is no match for Alexi, who, who is — ."

"Who is your lover you were on the verge of saying."

"Yes Momma."

"So you have lain with him?"

"Yes Momma."

"Then what else can I say? Nothing. I could cite scripture to you but won't. I can only hope and pray that you are not completely lost. Now, since I am at my wits end and can tell you nothing, let me ask my only daughter what she is to do next."

"Alexi and I have talked."

"Obviously. And of things that will whirl both of you upon ruin."

"Momma please let me finish."

Though perturbed she agreed. "All right."

"Alexi and I are planning a trip to a resort on the Adriatic north of here, where we'll spend two weeks in the sun and on the beaches together. Before that or soon afterwards we hope to marry, but there is first the divorce that must be approved by a court of law."

"Oh yes! Merely a slight hindrance! And where will you spend your hours and days waiting for the clearance that allows your marriage which will not be a thing of brevity I assure you?"

"Zagreb."

"The capitol of Croatia."

"Unh hunh."

"It's a terribly long way from Tirana here to Zagreb."

"It is. Five hundred seventy seven kilometers. A day's ride."

"I see. Why is he there?"

"He's training for a skate meet. He's to do it singly."

"With no partner?"

"No partner."

"You're traveling by train to meet him?"

"Oh yes Momma. That's the least expensive way."

"When will you leave?"

"In two days."

"Sergi Zakarov will be lonely. He is lonely it has come to me. He has recently taken an apartment here in Tirana since you left him. He paces the floor they say. Have you exchanged words with him with respect to your intentions?"

"That I'm leaving him?"

"Yes."

"I haven't but I will. I'll send a note. I don't want to hear his voice and I can't stand the thought of facing him."

"Have it as you like. I can't bless you. I'll pray that you come to your senses. How long are you to be away?"

"Indefinitely. We have talked of settling in that region."

Two days passed. As with all or most mothers she gave in to her daughter, yet declining to bestow her blessing, holding rigidly that the choice her daughter had made for herself was morally wrong. She avowed openly to no longer oppose her or interfere; even adding with loving tenderness that she'd help her pack and inquired if she had sufficient money for funding her journey and for living expenses during her stay. There sounded a thinly veiled hint in her tone that she expected it to be brief, yet resolved against bringing up the prospect. She said she'd go with her to catch the train, almost an insistence, and told her she loved her and kissed her cheek when Emanuelle politely mentioned that the hour was late and that she must get to bed. Her mother did not herself retire immediately, opting instead to sit for awhile at the kitchen table with only the candle glow as a companion, writing nonsensical figures on a tablet sheet over and over, thinking, thinking. At last she pushed her chair aside and stole softly into her daughter's bedroom and bent over her, pulling her up tightly, and kissed her good night a second time, then took to her own bed, careful to cover her face with her pillow so as not to let Emanuelle hear the sobbing. Sleep did not come easily, hardly at all. An old gentleman, her handyman, had lived down street for years, a good gentle neighbor and now she thought of him. He understood her torment, having listened to her pour out her distress for the past several days. Old and wise he had tried to console her.

"Young people are like that. They're headstrong. They make questionable decisions. It's a phase she's passing through. But just like tears do in time it'll dry up and go away."

Dark hung oppressively thick over the city when they left for the train station. The first from bed that morning her mother cooked breakfast, though not eating herself, claiming she wasn't hungry. The train would arrive early, that is, at five thirty, posing a hindrance at that hour to their seeing the obstacles that lay in front of them when stepping across the tracks to the passenger benches where Emanuelle would board her coach. Mother and daughter clung fast to each other, bracing themselves to avert tripping or falling.

"Careful! Don't lose your balance darling," one or the other said, taking time about to offer cautions, speaking louder than usual to overcome the unpleasant mix of screeching machinery and jaded voices of the yard workers who at times broke into hackneyed yells at one another.

The predawn mist had made its stealthy advent and was everywhere spread, not actually fog but behaving in the likeness of fog, enshrouding, dense, ominous, though its presence did not constitute the only impediment to the crowd standing around or sitting with coats pulled tightly against them. The coldness of the air met Emanuelle and her mother that morning the moment they left the old gentleman's car who drove them, nipping sharply at their skin, which forced a shiver from the two women, worsening now since they were sitting in stillness while waiting for the train to pull abreast. It could be seen down the tracks from their whereabouts a half block away, motionless, a sinister visage in the mist. It had stopped there, idling away time with no explainable reason for which everyone among the impatient crowd sought an answer, especially the younger ones.

"Why are they waiting like that? Why don't they come on?"

The headlight shone as a fiery red ball, while the exhaust ports of the monstrous mechanical spewed out jets of whitish angry steam which hissed with unmuffled vehemence. At last the engine coughed, then there were a series of jerks followed by a rattling as if the regimen of coaches were vibrating together all at once, and then the whole train began to creep forward until at length the engine rolled past them and kept rolling until the coach that Emanuelle would catch came even and got past as well, but only by a trifle then drew to a halt.

People of all ages and cultures were climbing off and onto the train, those climbing off of much greater numbers who to Emanuelle by far were the most intriguing. They were young males on military leave, largely, pouring into Tirana for the week end annual festival to be with their sweethearts who in spite of the unsavory coldness gathered on the station frontage to meet them. Young man and young woman rushed to each other, to happy hungry embraces and kisses and these sentiments, among still more, were mingled with whoops and cries of joy.

When the engine sent out its blast alerting the passengers to climb aboard Emanuelle together with her mother at once scrouged close to the boarding steps, both turning simultaneously to one another for the expected kiss and embrace, there lighting a moment afterwards on Emanuelle's face an expression suggesting she wished to say something intimately dear, though it failed to mature; and so she turned and hurriedly mounted the steps to the inside. She did not see her mother cry who now slowly began to cover the few paces to the old gentleman waiting to drive her home. Daylight had aggressively begun to push the darkness aside.

Leaving was not easy for the young girl, in fact much harder than she envisioned it would be, verified by the presence of a lump in her throat that she could not dislodge. She swallowed a time or two hoping that in doing so she might drive it away, which helped but the lump faintly remained. Settled in her seat now, she looked slowly around in expectation that some-one might join her, but there were a conglomeration of empty seats at that early hour, thereby squashing the likelihood that anyone would consider the attempt, choosing to sit alone. Soon the conductor came along, the first person she met, cheerily delivering a good morning greeting. He was a kindly man, she at once gathered, and his disposition impressed upon her that he favored in manner and movement the old gentleman who lived down street from her mother, both tall and trim with a propensity to talk lethargically slow when engaging in conversation. While she suffered the unfortunate emptiness of not ever seeing her father in real life she had kept a photograph of him on her bedroom credenza and thought the old conductor mirrored a shade of resemblance to him also.

"I see you're bound for Zagreb," he said drawlingly as he reached for her tickets in which he would punch holes with the silver pistol shaped device he held in his hand.

"Yes sir. An all day trip I've learned."

"You'll enjoy it. Lots of pretty things to see. Rivers and bridges and rugged mountainous areas, things like that."

"Yes sir. I'm sure I'll enjoy the scenery."

He cleared his throat, preparing to add one last thing.

"You might like to visit the diner Miss if you develop an appetite for coffee and breakfast. I think you'd enjoy that too."

"Thank you. In awhile maybe."

The conductor smiled, handed her tickets back, and made his way slowly down the aisle to ask others for their tickets as he had her. A detectable gleam of fondness showed in her eyes as they followed him, seemingly studying something appealingly special in the kindly fellow. And then clearing this away she turned to glance quickly at the people sitting in seats nearby, some dozing and some reading while others were busily preoccupied with whatever they saw through the window. She too decided to look out her window but almost wished she hadn't. There suddenly loomed Tirana in the distance, a half mile behind them, the idyllic little city a blink away from the sea coast of the Adriatic, visible now in that the train had begun to turn with the bend of the tracks. But not for long. She knew they would soon again straighten once the engine traveled far enough. She swallowed. The lump in her throat had come back.

"How tiny my Tirana seems to be from here. I will miss it. I already miss it and I've hardly left. I grew up there; I've lived my life there. How could I not miss it?"

Then she caught a glimpse of the aged Saint Procopius Church towering above the dwellings and business structures around it, a church she had attended since her baptismal as a baby by the Holy Father of the Orthodox faith, "the old priest, who I have daily met at mass ever since I can remember and he's still there. He always puts his arm around me when I enter the doorway and seems to utter a special blessing in language I cannot make out." She recalled as well her most intimate friends, girls her age, going all the way back to childhood. When reaching teenage years they'd parade the streets of downtown and venture into the serried shops and kioshs which sold every variety of collectible, among these cowboy hats and ball point pins. "What memorable days," the reflection ran through her, a pensive smile settling on her face.

The trees and houses rushed by and soon they penetrated into open country, the houses now far and few between, and Tirana many miles behind. She glanced about at the passengers, as she often did, most still asleep, and a few still reading. She fretted. "Why did I not bring a magazine or an interesting book? That distresses me. I knew I'd forget something." It came to her that the conductor suggested she might like to visit the diner, an enticement that pressed hard upon her to fulfill but she would not indulge just then, in awhile. She would take a nap for the time being, only a short one and on this impulse adjusted her seat to a comfortable recline and lay back, and tried to fall asleep which refused to come, the fault traceable to the low smooth rumble of the swaying coach and the rhapsodic sound of the wheels that rolled upon the tracks of pressed steel that supported them. The clacking tempo kept receding into the drowsy stillness of early morning, such that eventually it proved to be more than wakefulness could bear and so she toppled over, not hearing the conductor call out the name of a small town they were approaching where they would stop and take on and let off passengers, nor did she hear the whistle of the engine when the engineer ritualistically signaled good morning and waved to a farmer and his wife in the rural countryside sitting on their front porch waiting to wave back. At spaced intervals heavy billowing puffs of thick black smoke burst from the emission stack of the engine, a reminder of the stupendous work output of this great machine and that with every puff moved closer to Emanuelle's destination. Passers by on their way to the diner slyly stole a peek at the lovely sleeping girl with the short tossed salad hairdo, a sizeable many of them women, who drooled and envied a style they seldom saw. It set her apart. Sergi Zakarov recommended it for her skating meets. Suddenly she awakened, at once realizing that the train had covered a span of extended length as she slept, perhaps passing through several small towns whose names she wouldn't have recognized even if she'd heard the conductor call them out. She wondered how far they had come and became aware as she looked across the way that the landscape was now changing, gradually rising and falling, but mostly rising, and that the foothills of the mountains were looming in the distance which the old conductor had foretold. Wondrous as these shrines of nature were they proved to be only of ephemeral attraction, giving way to things more humanly swaying, remembrances of the old priest and the Saint Procopius Church and how he always hugged her and gave her irreverent attention, of her mother so saddened at seeing her leave, of Tirana itself and its many aspects — the holiday festivals, the dances on the open square on weekends, the beaches where she'd lie for long stretches with girls her age basking in the sun while listening to the radio, the carefree high school days, standing and watching the sea waves crashing and dissolving on the shoreline, and the beginnings of her learning to skate, all these, among a rash of others. But there was as well that sinking feeling that subtly once more invaded her stomach. She couldn't repress it. She would struggle with herself, reasoning back and forth.

"Oh dear me. Not now. Don't tell me I'm feeling a tinge of loneliness. But I am. I admit it. I didn't tell her but it just about broke my heart when I left my Momma at the station and it almost broke hers too.

Oh stop it. You'll only be away for awhile. You've left many times before like this and you weren't sad then.

It's true. I wasn't sad. Well, I was some. I was always a little. But the truth is I didn't think I'd start to feel lonely this quickly.

You'll be all right. As the day wears on and the bright sun rises higher you'll start to enjoy yourself and forget these plaguing things trying to pull you down."

Behind them now lay Gjonem, Lezhe, and Shkoder, three fairly large populaces, and Podgorica across the border in Montenegro stood next in line, where as in the case of other towns it would stop again to let passengers on and off and drop the sacks of mail to which the rural folks looked forward with mounting anticipation. The sun at this hour had escalated to midmorning height, thereby sending a radiance of warmth through the window of Emanuelle's coach and onto her lovely face. She should have felt buoyed over this pleasant occurrence of nature but to her discovery that did not happen. Nor did she look at the pretty streams and bright landscape that begged to be beheld and envied by encompassing eyes.

The sinking feeling in her stomach now was even more apparent and she commenced to reflect on the cause and on a means of ridding herself of the aggravation. She should be happy, she reasoned, and reproached herself for not being so, for Alexi Konstanty at the end of the line in Zagreb anxiously and happily awaited her arrival, she assumed, as they had pre planned. So she started with him and continued to keep him presently of mind for some considerable miles, visiting and revisiting their past and present connection with each other. It would take awhile.

"Alexi is a lovely person. And so gorgeous. I fell in love with him the moment Sergi Zakarov introduced us, 'Emanuelle, this is Alexi Konstanty, your new skating partner,' and when we finished with our first whirl around the arena I knew that I could not resist falling in love with him. Moving as smoothly as a swan he looked smilingly down into my eyes and I smiled caressingly back, knowing then by the feeling that swept over me that my emotions were hopelessly bound. Still, I must confess, I'm not in love with him as much as once I was, nor do I think his heart flutters as madly as once it did when he sets eyes on me. So I must ask: is it possible that in the end, after we've lived together for awhile, we will discover that our love, our affection, will have seriously waned and then go our separate ways, which I don't believe will fall as hard upon him as it will me. Why then, if I now think these things, am I on this trip racing to meet him? Perhaps it is too easy to explain to myself that I simply am and let it go at that, and that thousands of women have done the same, which is no excuse for me. Is it also as my Momma said, that I am mixed up, as well as Alexi Konstanty? Have I erred so badly? If my union with Alexi were to fail it would then be my second marriage to have crashed upon the rocks. And only his first. Besides, my sins are greater than his; he is not a married person, and yet, I am and I have sinned with him, I a married woman. I have lain with him. I even admitted this to my Momma. Oh, the look of shock in her face. She later cried, believing she hid it from me. And what if I had gotten with child? Would he have stuck by me, would he? The fact that this unpleasant image visits my head, this awful possibility, means that there is some measure of apprehension astir that he would not. What has he to lose? He is a free man and I am a married woman. Oh how worrisome these dark specters that bear upon me. But there is one more. I wonder if he ever looks at someone other than me. Ha! Wasted question. He's a man isn't he?"

But Alexi Konstanty did not exist as the sole person on which her concentration dwelled. The image of the good father of Saint Procopius began to reemerge.

"While I've not given it much concern of late I have observed that my dear old priest has not embraced me nor said those angelic uplifting words at the doorway when I attend mass. His manner is cool and unfriendly. How naive I am. He has heard, as others have, that I am no longer with Sergi Zakarov and that I have favored someone else who has captured my heart. No wonder his gentle eyes have lost their warmth and affection. I have sinned. I am a sinner, and likely will soon receive formal announcement that I am presently forbade a place in church, which I deserve."

The mighty train sped northward, its horn blasting at every crossing, the engineer waving his hands with unabated relish at the people who did likewise at him. Eventually, one by one as they approached them, Emanuelle heard the old conductor call out first Niksic, then Trebinje, and then Makarska, quaint colorful towns or cities hundreds of years old nestled at an agreeable setback from the railroad track which bore marks that once the ancient Romans and in later centuries the Ottoman Turks were unwelcome yet resourceful occupants. The train had crossed over to the eastern shore of Croatia where the blue waters of the Adriatic glistened playfully in the sun and for a stretch Emanuelle drank in the lushness of the scenery, almost forgetting her worries. But this was of short duration.

She returned once more to the rather uncomfortable clash with her mother two nights before she left Tirana to meet Alexi Konstanty. It had nothing to do with her being mixed up as her mother said; it was attendant to her father, her mother's husband, of his goodness, a wondrously good man, who saved her life, and by so doing paved the way for the birth of their daughter into this world. She had said to her daughter that Sergi Zakarov possessed profoundly good qualities as well and patterns of character that strikingly resembled those of her husband.

"It seems I've dwelled upon everyone but him. So what about him, I ask myself? He is a good man. I cannot dispute that. And has done much for me. Let me see. Let me go back. He was young when he first moved to Tirana, and very handsome, and is now even still but older. He'd left Russia for a warmer climate and Tirana appealed to his fancy. I remember how the young girls my age took on over him when he showed up at the beach clad in nicely fitting swimming shorts and sporting a sexy physique. His hair set him off most, bulky, black, with a curl that hung down a tad in front. That's where I first saw him, at the beach. Someone spoke of him as a famous skater and that caught my interest right off. I lived and breathed to be a great skater, not believing for a second that I ever could or would. I heard that he sometimes put on ice skating demonstrations at the skating rink, so I started going over there to see them and afterwards would skate myself, and that is specifically where I met him. I had gone there since childhood, taken by my mother who saw benefit in me starting early. He took notice of me right away, half stumbling, half skating, in my eyes anyway, but not in his apparently, for one day, finally, by some miracle he whizzed over and invited me to skate a round or two with him. He seemed literally to float, skating to him as natural as the human breath or a bird flying. Then when we finished he asked me to skate around on the ice for a stretch alone, mostly in circles, he directed, and when he saw enough he signaled to me to halt and skated over. I prayed for his approval.

'You have promise,' I remember him saying in a congratulatory tone, and not long thereafter I began to seriously train under his watchful guise. In time I became proficient, skating with the finest of skaters, and eventually attained to stardom."

She paused, pondering, on the verge of saying next that she met Alexi Konstanty on the ice too, though suddenly acquired a decisiveness not to utter his name. She wished as well that her thoughts of Sergi Zakarov would go away, but they wouldn't, which she admitted to herself on second consideration that she didn't want them to go away, but that there were many things more she must work through.

"He is a good man. I know that. Momma said he did a lot for me, making me the best on ice to be sure, but there is more than that to speak of. We spent two joyful years in that little white bungalow by the sea and then he bought a bigger home, where I lived until recently. It too is situated on the sea, just higher up in the hills. Our lives were of the purest happiness. I can't deny that. I can't. I won't. We'd often go out for dinner on the sea front. Sometimes we'd talk while eating, sometimes not at all. There ran a strain of quietness in him which I learned to anticipate and came to inordinately respect. It suggested wisdom and depth of thought. After we'd eaten we'd walk along the promenade talking and looking at the strange reddish streaks over the waters, the magical doing of the late setting sun. In the evening when the wind had calmed and the night had fallen we'd pick out a spot on the pier where we could see the twinkling steamers gliding their way in. We'd then set out for practice. He could skate forever despite having dropped below the crest of his prime. He never tired. He'd tell me to take time out and rest or he'd take me home and rub me until I felt no more aches and pains. I loved many things in our life together, but more I think the Sunday mornings when we went to mass. Everybody knew us, everybody loved us. And Momma spilled over with pride. We were married in that church, Sergi Zakarov and I, by the same dear old priest that we still have."

The repentance that now began to course though her did not evolve without pain and remorse, which commenced as a vague and gnawing uneasiness, a sinking feeling, that past early morning when she kissed her mother goodbye, increasingly bothersome as the day and miles lengthened, until finally she gave up and let go, unable to longer hold it all in and so began a litany of self questioning, sorrowful regrets, and hopes that she could be forgiven.

"Ah what have I done? Where did I get lost? Why did my wings fly so far from the nest? When did I turn blind? Can I ever find my way back to the man I know now I dearly and truly love, who loves me more than he loves himself? Is the life I once knew and cherished gone from me for good? Is the chance passed forever for me to bear and raise his children, watching them grow up with him at my side, with the best father they could ever have and the best husband that ever was? What kind of fool is it that would give up all this? What kind of fool is it that will trade love for passion? I have met that fool. It is I. Will God ever forgive me? Will Sergi Zakarov ever take me back? What can I do? Perhaps Momma will know."

At this the old conductor on seeing the forlornness of the young woman stopped off to inquire if something bothered her, if an illness might have descended.

"Can I be of help to you Miss? You look a mite distraught."

"When will the train be stopping sir?"

"Twenty minutes from now. Did you need to stop before then? An emergency of some sort?"

"No sir. Nothing like that. Only that I need to get off there. I'm going back home."

"I see. You'll need to catch the next train south I'm assuming. If my memory serves me correctly it's the only one traveling in that direction for the rest of the day. It leaves the station thirty minutes after this one leaves heading north."

"Thank you. Do they have a telephone there that I could use?"

"I am certain they do. If you'll call collect."

"Momma, Momma," she cried out as she heard her mother's sweet and excited voice on the other end of the line, "I'm coming home. I'm coming home."

"What on earth darling? Are you hurt, are you sick?"

"No Momma. I've just made a terrible mistake, that's all. I'll explain when I get there. I'm catching the train for Tirana very shortly. I'll arrive in the vicinity of six o'clock. In the meantime will you do something for me?"

"Of course. What darling?"

"Tell Sergi not to go out to eat this evening which I know he has started to do. Tell him to please wait. Tell him that I'm coming home and will be there in time to cook his supper."

Sojourn To Emporia

"TOMMY, TOMMY!" I heard Elvin excitedly calling my name. I had attained to eleven years of age and had made countless friends at the orphanage. Elvin Hawthorne was number one; we were inseparable, even successfully persuading the supervisor to let us do odd jobs together on the farm, and even our cots abutted where we slept in the barracks with twenty or so other boys, talking, whispering that is, forever of home or where it used to be late into the night.

The orphanage, a Christian dwelling was established in the century preceding by a collectivity of church denominations whose vision placed it in the small frontier town of Guymon, Oklahoma, although I fail to pinpoint when. None of the denominations in particular exercised singular control or influence, the primary affairs of governance resting in the hands of Bradford Warren, the superintendent, an able executive possessing the rare ability to know when to show sternness and when to apply a well deserved pat on the back. The children were fortunate to have him.

I had gone to the barn earlier that morning to see after one of the mares in foal when soon after, Elvin, breathless, came running in.

"What is it?"

"Tommy, Tommy!"

"What's wrong Elvin?"

"Your daddy's here!"

"You joke."

"I'm not kidding. It's true. Your daddy is here. He's in Mr. Warren's office right now."

I saw he wasn't kidding. My father, John B. Devine had come back. I could not believe what I heard. It was now 1941, five years having passed since last I saw him. No letters, no nothing. I lay awake nights wondering if he were still alive, wondering if I might ever see him and my brothers and sisters again. At times I got so angry. "Why did he just give us away, me and Harold and Brady? Didn't he love us?" Even after Harold's patient explanation I felt the same.

"Do you think you'll be leavin' here?" Elvin anxiously asked. So much spun in my head that his babbling shot by me. .

My eyes moved with studious scrutiny over the young mare lying before me on the earthen barn floor, to which over time I became infinitely attached and believed, yet couldn't begin to comprehend how, she in an animal sense held equal fondness for me. I knew she needed my help. As I rubbed my hand across her protruding belly she stared at me with bright amber eyes and appeared to be relieved. I assumed so.

"Tommy, did you hear me? Your daddy's here and Harold and Brady are with him right now." Harold and Brady, my brothers, were admitted to the orphanage with me, Harold the oldest and I the youngest.

"They're with Mr. Warren. I'll bet he's here to take ya'll home."

I did not answer; rather, I stood, wiped the sweat from my brow and lit out for the superintendent's office. "We were left here by our father," the thought pounded through my head, "and literally he tore me away from him, a mere child, frightened and angry and bursting with heartache." The lingering agony of it did not easily go away. For awhile I presumed he outright deserted us, but began to judge differently after Harold repeatedly, detail by detail, went over the circumstances. I am unknowledgeable of my age when it seriously struck me but eventually as I matured enough to assess my own youthful obstinacy, and my father's pitiable plight; I felt a very private humiliating shame.

Left with eight children to feed, clothe, and care for when they were sick, he must have looked in on himself and saw a man profoundly helpless. I suppose that is why he soon married again. My real mother Gladys Marie Devine died in 1932, two years before, when I was just age two, and although he couldn't see or suspect it the future promised to worsen. His new wife brought to the household three children of her own, therefore, our family grew from eight children to eleven children and a father and stepmother. The relationship with her and her children began to deteriorate from the start, destined never to work out. She was pretty but swollen with disgruntlement, and intolerable for us to be around. Her thin taut lips and cold brown eyes exposed a spiteful demeanor. Not infrequently she wore a frown, finding it grudgingly impossible to smile. It was glaringly seen that she favored her own over the rest, a logical attitude to have expected, but it might have behooved her to show more kindness toward us inasmuch as a separation and divorce from my father lurked imminently in the making. I suspect with the most of certainty that her ill treatment of his children, whom he loved dearly, led to the breach.

It seemed that nothing we did proved right. Everything displeased her. Since I was the youngest of the Devine clan I am sure that things weren't as hard for me. But the older boys caught her wrath and for awhile my father failed to detect the antipathy she held for them in her breast.

Working long hours in the wheat and cotton fields kept him away during the day and consequently unable to witness the inconsiderate treatment of my brothers. Once in particular, Harold and one of our stepbrothers ended up in a tussle. It happened in late afternoon, near suppertime, that the stepbrother slipped into the house a short while before and snitched an apple. The children were forbidden to take even a crumb without asking permission. Harold threatened to expose him if the fruit went unshared. A scuffle ensued and just before our stepmother emerged from the house our stepbrother tossed the apple to Harold which he caught, and also caught it from her who adjudged him to be the thief, not her son.

"Harold Devine, you awful boy. You know you're not supposed to be eatin' anything without my permission." Acting on principle Harold decided to take a flogging rather than squeal on his stepbrother and the flogging got underway. She started switching him. But then my father suddenly showed up.

"What's going on here?"

"This awful son of yours is making trouble as usual."

Harold figured it useless to explain the fracas to his father, partially because he realized that our stepmother would go to far reaching extremes before admitting the truth, even if she knew it. That night, in private, my father asked Rhonda for her explanation of the cause of it all. If anything came from the lips of Rhonda it in my father's reasoning amounted to undisputable.testimony. A short while thereafter my stepmother and three children moved out.

We lived in Aurora, Kansas which when translated means first light. He clung desperately to a small farm that he and my mother purchased in 1921 with the help of the bank, but the depression a decade or more later spread widely across the land, work nowhere to be found and people unable to maintain mortgage requirements. Upon failure to meet payments foreclosure descended swiftly. In the instance of my father the long painful years of trying to pay off his loan went down the drain. All was lost! Sitting morosely on the edge of his farm — but no longer under his ownership — he watched while row after row of corn and cotton were plowed under that he himself planted, ordered by the banker who in taking custody of the property capitalized exorbitantly from the destruction of the crops. So as to curtail excessive planting — the cause of dangerous falls in the prices of farm commodities — the government with good intentions instituted a practice of subsidizing farmers for holding back or cutting back production acreage. My father held his hands over his face as he sat and cried. Seeing him weep as he did sent trickles of numbness throughout my body and a never before experienced weakness rushed to my stomach, forcing me to lean over and drop to my knees.

When, after the passage of years, now rearing children of my own, he responded to a belated letter that I prepared and sent which expressed sorrow over his bad luck. His words touched my heart.

> Dear Son,
>
> Do not shoulder a burden that bodes no gain to anyone. Please! Do not fret or grieve over my misfortune, a dream, you say, fallen apart. We had our dream, son, your mother and me. Oh yes! We planned; we talked; we played; we envisioned something grand; we built an empire with our imagination: cattle grazing in lush green meadows, masses of land (our own) sprawling clear to the horizon; and a splendid two story

> home atop the highest rise large enough to raise a family of twenty children.
>
> Dreams! Ah, how we dreamed. But don't you see? It is forever so that striving toward a dream is far more thrilling than the attainment of it.

So now Elvin was telling me that my father arrived a short while ago, at last making his way back to the orphanage. This was the day I'd waited and hoped for but my feelings troubled me. While on our way to Mr. Warren's office Elvin hammered me with one question after another, none of which I can be confident I answered. As we stepped onto the veranda the screen door flew open and out ran Brady.

"Our daddy's home. He got here just a little bit ago. He's gonna take us home with him. He's moved. He lives in Emporia. Got a good job too. We don't live in Aurora anymore. He's married again too. Her name's Dollie. Dollie Devine. Doncha think its pretty. It's like a rhyme. Says we'll like her a lot."

Wild with excitement Brady talked so rapidly that I hardly comprehended his words and must have appeared dazed because he put his hands on my shoulders and literally shook me back and forth. "Tommy, didji hear me?"

"Married!" It hit me joltingly. "Why on earth?" I mumbled to myself, the turmoil we experienced with our first stepmother swirling in my head. "Are we in for that again?"

"Tommy! Didji hear me?" No, I did not hear him. My thoughts were exploding. All this a bit complicated for a youngster to handle, my father suddenly showing up from out of the blue and news of another stepmother.

"Yes," I finally answered, my mouth dry and voice suffering from hoarseness which I took resulted from the surge of excitement. At that instant, seeing someone standing in the doorway I recognized him, my father. Streaks of gray coursed through his hair, receding faintly into his temples, and there was a bearing of having aged a few years but otherwise, with vibrant eyes and wind tanned skin, he looked the picture of health. He stood there, kind of fixated, just looking me over, with tears glistening in his eyes and for a moment gave the impression that he'd lost the capability of thinking of something to say. As he came hurriedly to me and threw his arms around me I suddenly felt the pint up anger lift from my heart.

"Tommy, my how you've grown, so tall and handsome. I hardly knew you," he uttered, choking up and pulling me tighter to him. His hand affectionately squeezed my shoulder, the one I tried desperately to hold onto years ago when he left us at the orphanage doorway. It seemed a lifetime. As I looked into his face, almost straight across, I saw the love I so wanted to know was there during the years of his absence. .

"Daddy, are you really here to take us home?"

"Yes son I am. I've so longed for this day. You don't know how badly."

Did the days since we last saw one another pass as slowly for him as for me? I presumed so. But it only mattered that he made his way back at last. We went into Mr. Warren's office and took our seats, while Elvin, sticking like glue watched absorbingly and bent forward from his chair, anxiously making certain that he missed nothing.

"Boys let me have your attention. We need to talk," Mr. Warren said kindly.

We sat erect and grew stone quiet. .

"Your dad and I talked before we sent for you and decided there are some things we should go over."

"Yes my sons," my father added, "you have been here for five years and life outside this orphanage will be quite a change. You'll have to get used to a different kind of freedom."

Freedom! That word rang loudly in my head: no waiting in line for meals, no nine o'clock bedtime check, no showering with scores of other boys, no morning and afternoon chores, no sleeping in an open barracks with twenty others.

Finally, Mr. Warren's voice came through again. "Yes, life will be somewhat different. You've gained a great deal while you've been with us. No doubt you've learned discipline, responsibility, and cooperation, and although blessed with a strong spiritual background on your entry here, I'm sure it has matured into even a more serious faith. You have praiseworthy morals, I know that for sure. Tommy, on occasions you were quizzed in respect to particular occurrences that troubled me. You always told the truth, even when to your disadvantage, and I greatly appreciated that. Honesty with your fellow man can take you a long way in life and boys this I say to all of you. The years you've lived here are a part of your past, your history, and they will always stay with you. Use what you have learned wisely and make us proud as well as yourselves. Well, you have a long trip ahead, so I suggest you start to pull your things together. Mr. Devine here tells me he plans to leave first thing tomorrow morning."

During the talk between Mr. Warren and my father, Elvin and I sat side by side trading glances, the expression on his face telling me what went on in his heart. We were so close for a very long time, but now only a few hours away from separating and doing so wouldn't come easily. What could I say to him? Soon I would leave and he would remain.

"Daddy, can Elvin come to see us sometime? He's my best friend."

Something stole across Elvin's face, something of a mixed description, pride, joy, importance. "My best friend! That's what he said about me." I'm sure those were the thoughts running through him.

"Of course he can Tommy. We always have room for one more. Maybe Mr. Warren can work something out for Elvin to ride the train over to Emporia to see us."

"I think that's a possibility," Mr. Warren replied, suddenly emitting an unexpected grin, which, likened to my father, did not reflect his usual character.

Elvin and I were in seventh heaven at the prospect of his visit, but fought to hold back tears as we hugged, realizing that a final goodbye was on its way. At a later period, a few years as I swept back upon the scene, it stirred within me with sobering appreciation that Mr. Warren and my father did all within them to help two young boys struggle through a difficult farewell.

As planned, we left early the next morning, the air cool and moist and the sun not yet rising. With sights trained eastward we set out in father's second hand 1934 Ford, a rickety old vehicle of questionable operating capability in that there lay ahead of us a long grinding span before reaching our destination. We would follow a straight eastward course through Oklahoma until aligning with Emporia on the north, or thereabouts, then turn acutely in that direction, soon crossing into the state of Kansas. It was calculated that on the whole we would meet with the better road conditions if going along that route way instead of choosing other options which, as my father saw it, would have meant fewer miles of travel. But again he worried over the old car's ability to withstand the least of hazards and thus abandoned any course other than the one which he previously charted.

We, the three boys, sat in the back seat, the top let down, folded in place onto the upper edge of the storage trunk. My father and a friend, who sat beside him, a robust man of ruddy complexion with a prizefighter nose jammed against his face, were to share the driving. Harold whispered that the man came along to help my father, gladdened news, for we all knew that there were fifteen, maybe sixteen hours ahead of us. Maybe more. And that we could expect slow travel.

"Boys, this is Mr. Bigham, Mr. Willie Bigham. He's going to help me drive during the trip."

"How you doin' boys?" Mr. Bigham spoke out in a voice both deep and friendly, twisting his head around so as to see us more directly.

"We couldn't be better Mr. Bigham," answered Harold, "we're going home."

"Brady! Tommy! I didn't hear from you." my father spoke up..

"Oh yes, Mr. Bigham, we're fine."

As we discovered Mr. Bigham proved to be a tremendously jovial man, profusely chuckling while telling a hodgepodge of stories and pouncing with relish on any story irrespective of who brought it up or its apparent insignificance. His presence greatly helped in making the trip more pleasant. You might have taken him to be outright pompous if meeting him for the first time, but you would have seen him wrongly. We discovered him to be earthly funny and buoyant. A somber quiet man my father seldom said anything, consistently lost in thought. We were not long on the road when he pulled over for a check of the oil level, uttering in barely audible phrases better to be safe than sorry. Assuming it his duty, Mr. Bigham slid out and began to circle around the car in the semblance of an animal positioning to attack a prey, narrowing his eyes at every tire and tread, taking care to the point of incisive scrutiny that things were as they should be. Satisfied, he leaned against the fender and gave it an affectionate pat.

"You're a Brave Heart," he said, as if speaking to an actual human. "Yes sir! You're a Brave Heart." I stood nearby, curious, amused.

"What did you call it?"

"A Brave Heart. That's what I called it."

"Ahhh!"

"You see Tommy, this old crate is more than a jumble of connected metal parts and rubber tires that roll on the ground. Yes sir? Why in a way, more than you could guess, it's human. Did you know that? And the more you hang around it the more human it gits." Mr. Bigham was putting on a show.

"I'll declare," I let out, pretending astonishment. "Do you think it can stand the trip to Emporia?"

"Shoot! You can rely on it. I learned that on the way out here. It'll get us there son. Yes sir. I listened to it real good. A mite noisy, but it's got powerful will power. "

The horseplay excepted, I understood the seriousness of his point. To be certain, everyone to the last man and boy depended on how well the aging jalopy could endure the strains that lay coiled in wait. As we penetrated deeper into the journey we came to think of it as a genuine member of the family. Although no one said as much. That it assumed an inordinately indispensable role no one doubted, and from there on Brave Heart became the official name by which we addressed it.

"Let's go," I heard my father call out in warm yet soldierly tone, and soon we were on the road, the occupants in the back still wild with excitement, frantically swiveling their necks so as to catch sight of all things in all directions all at once. There could not have been a more beautiful day for traveling.

"I'm so happy," Brady practically squealed. Harold and I were thrilled as much and echoed his feelings.

"So am I," we said together, both our father and Mr. Bigham nodding gladly.

But Harold nudged me lightly with his elbow and when I looked into his eyes I saw them at once excited and sad, and it puzzled me.

"What's the matter?"

He spoke in a whisper, in a lowness that allowed only Brady and me to hear.

"It's strange."

"Strange! I don't know what you mean" I said, truly unable to decipher what he in the least intimated. But did as he said more.

"It's strange. It's like we ought to be going back to where we came from, to Aurora." He sighed. "You know what I mean. That's where we were born. That's where mother died."

His melancholy stare tailed off into the obscurity, a rueful stare perhaps better said. I wished I could lessen his sadness but counseled myself that temporary silence could only be the best medicine to prescribe, so I let it go at that. Seeing him lost in distant ponder I settled upon a rash of ideas and thoughts myself, and continued in this vein until the remembrance of my father's marriage to Dollie reappeared which gnawed at me relentlessly ever since hearing the news of it from Brady.

"Harold, I'm not going to like our stepmother, I just know it."

"Why do you say that?"

"You know how stepmother's are."

"How?"

"They don't like stepchildren."

"Tommy, daddy says she's different. She can't wait to see us, and she loves our brothers and sisters who are with her now in Emporia. And what's more, they love her too."

But the exchange between us started to fade and his thoughts returned straightaway to where they were previously.

"Tommy, what do you remember about Aurora?"

My original whereabouts on this earth was in the vicinity of Aurora, Kansas, a little known town northeast of the orphanage by something like three hundred fifty miles in Cloud County, where I lived with my family for a short time in a dust whipped farm house when my mother still lived, then later during my father's marriage to his second wife. A poor specimen for accommodating a family the old house fell as time rolled by into a condition badly wanting, yet so too were the mass of family dwellings throughout the region. It consisted of four rooms with high plain ceilings which were heated by a round cast iron wood devouring stove. The water supply we drew from a backyard well situated next to the back porch, and an outhouse swept off to the south by a considerable distance. When my father remarried, our family of siblings, together with the three brought to him by his new wife summed to eleven children, as elsewhere noted, and the two adults added a ratio in excess of three persons per room, including the kitchen. Pallets spread onto the coarse foot worn floors were commonly utilized as makeshift beds. Living conditions were abysmally crowded, agonizingly uncomfortable, and at night you could hear someone forever sniffling, coughing, or crying. The wind during the biting months of winter leapt fiercely through the gaping clapboard cracks and loose fitting window jams, drastically chilling the inside air, thereby making it necessary to feed the stove with exacting regularity.

"Daddy, it's cold," I recall Rhonda crying out, the oldest of the siblings. She worried more for her younger brothers and sister than for herself. With our real mother gone Rhonda inherited her instinct of caring for the young.

"I'll take care of it darling. Musn't let the children get cold, no sir."

Picking up an arm full of wood chunks he pitched them through the yawning mouth of the monstrously large cast iron stove, then stirred vigorously with the poker. And waited. "Bhrrooom." The flames leapt savagely and then as they subsided into an attitude of calm my father went back to bed. Clad in long johns he depicted in the shadowy glow a jovial Santa Claus figure, the garment sticking to him as if he were melted and poured into it. Since the children slept close together we began to whisper how funny he looked, until at length a symphony of youthful giggles escaped from under the covers which we pulled up over our faces to keep him from hearing, though the effort proved futile.

"All right kidos! What's going on?"

"Nothing."

He knew better, and obviously enjoyed the playfulness. Abruptly, someone burst out again, too full to hold back. Eventually, when our cavorting reached a stage of excess — .

"Okay. Time to go to sleep."

Why did fate not allow him more time with us, more time to play with us? The struggle to keep a job, the effort to keep going, what weighty burdens, I thought at that early age, as I do presently. How trying the struggle to rear a family of such prodigious size during an era of American history characterized by brutally hard times. By all accounts the great depression wreaked havoc, immense tragedy, and in the manner of scores of other fathers, mine was grippingly trapped by it. In my thoughts of that dear one there is a consummate sorrow in my heart and to this day the occasions are frequent when I utter a little prayer that in his waning years he knew peace and rest and comfort, at least a morsel of reward for his troubles.

Invariably there occurred nightly biological needs. I'd rise twice during the night at the minimum to relieve myself. At first I started the process by standing on the edge of the back porch, with Gary standing by my side to assure that I didn't fall off. But my father after awhile altered the location of toiletry. "Gary," he sleepily yawned, "go with him, see that he gets on away from the house when he leaks." Ultimately I conditioned myself to roll out immediately when the urge struck, concerned that I might lapse into sleep and wet the quilts and mattress on which I slept, which would have been dreadfully embarrassing. I could have used the chamber, the "pot," which the women of the family used, yet for a reason akin to the concept of manliness, the males of the family usually initiated bladder relief in the yard, irrespective of the season.

With the advent of summer it became common for the bulk of the family to drop quilts onto the front porch flooring for our nightly sleep, in that on the inside the bedrooms were swelteringly hot. We did our best at warding off mosquitoes.

Burdened with the encumbrance of aging, treated in all likelihood with not the best of nurture in its former life, Brave Heart spat and belched when confronted with climbing a grade, pfffch, pitit, pfffch, pitit, bang, backfiring with a thunderous noise, thus evoking hilarious laughter among its young occupants.

"It don't like to climb no hill!" Mr. Bigham injected. There were no hills in Western Oklahoma, only vast plains with undulating rolls stretching to infinity, with tiny unpainted houses and barns sporadically dotting the landscape. A faded windmill could be seen popping up every once in awhile, groaning in resistance to the unceasing wind while ahead a round brackish object rolled across the narrow snaking roadway, followed by another and still another. A chase of some sort was going on. When we got closer I recognized that what I saw was a sortie of uprooted tumbleweeds, ugly and parched, and brittle — a full one year since they deceased — having broken loose from the fields where they grew in uncountable supply. I gazed as a hawk at the vastness of the landscape, its wonders, its haunting beauty; a country bountifully rewarding or harshly restricting. It ran in my knowledge for the first time that this trip, this sojourn, was symbolic of a man's life, for what was a man's life but a sojourn, a trip likened to the one on which we now embarked, which begins and moves and keeps moving, further and further away from that exact spot and date of its beginning, progressing to that unavoidable certainty — the end, which is impossible to contemplate as to where and when.

My father and his friend chatted for the most part with respect to the dust storms and the depression. I looked always for an opportunity to worm in.

"Is it dusty around Emporia?"

"Well son I — ."

My father did not finish. Mr. Bigham cut in.

"Shucks yeah. But it's soon gone."

"Where to?"

"Where does it go? Why boy, it lands over here in Oklahoma, then you know what?"

"No sir."

"Well, the very next day it blows back over in Kansas, square dab in the middle of Emporia. Ha, ha, ha, ha, ha." He slapped my father's shoulder. I liked him, and so did my father. He was a true self, frankly friendly, a man kindly inclined and a sage in his own fashion. Seeing them together like that, two men of gentle hearts and completely agreeable affinities brought to me that there were no two better men anywhere, and recalled in the same breath, "Good company and good discourse are the very sinews of virtue."

Then Mr. Bigham went on telling a substantially less fantastic story, yet one which compellingly attracted the back seat occupants whose ears strained to hear the whole of it. "Well boys, Emporia is different. Sure is. Little town is pocketed in a valley. Well, I guess its sort of a low place. Real fertile. Runs on up all the way to Canada. They grow wheat there, good tall stuff, and good cattle raisin's there too. Not to mention dairying."

"Wheat?" I queried. "You say it grows all the way to Canada?"

"Sure does. I've worked it all the way up there. Course it grows with the climate, the time of year."

"Whataya mean by that?"

"It's like this. The season starts early somewhere down in Texas. Later, a mite to the north, to around Amarillo, another phase of the harvest begins to come into its own. After that it begins to move into Oklahoma, then into Kansas, and clear on up into Canada. Saskatchewan! That's where it all grinds to a halt. Right there. End of the run."

I tapped him on his shoulder. "I wanna work the wheat fields too when I grow up."

Mr. Bigham's eyes glinted and showed arousal at the unstudied impractical sense of my ambition. "Son, that's mighty tough work. Makes a man old before his time. Do something else."

Unexpectedly my father started telling of his venture with the wheat harvesters and after he finished I felt certain that Mr. Bigham had offered some carefully forethought advice. In exacting detail he reconstructed how for a few months he followed the incessant movement of men and machines across the open plains in the naked fierce heat of summer, revealing that in some men there is an irrepressible endurance and power of will to go on when they at times believe there's not another step left in them.

"As I look back on it there are two things that stand out most about the wheat harvest; the terribly hard work and the suppertime meals. From sun up till sun down we toiled. Strong backs labored in the sweltering heat, some falling by the wayside and others staying with the task — sweating, straining, aching, suffering — swearing they were quitting. When the day ended we dragged ourselves to the bunkhouse, washed our faces and bodies with water freshly drawn from the well and made our way to the feeding hall, a shed, where we threw ourselves upon the supper the Mexican cook had set out on crude oaken tables. The scene was hardly better than barbaric. To the left and right of me men snatched for this or that, ravenously crunching and swallowing, constantly reaching for more drink or more beef or more bread or more beans. There was something of a rhythm to it all, thirty or forty jaws devouring the food in simultaneous togetherness. It wasn't supper. It was a primitive feast.

It amazed me that I held on as long as I did. If the wheat run had lasted another two days I would have dropped out. I would work the wheat fields again from time to time, but never with the corporation crews; only for farmer friends here and there."

The roads were of varying conditions, stretches embedded of either hardtop or gravel, or sometimes only miles of convoluted reddish dirt. We worried more about the effects of gravel than anything else, not infrequently my father expressing concern, but never using profanity, "Doggone rocks are gonna cause a blowout. I can feel it."

"Sure would hate to git bogged down here in the middle of nowhere," Mr. Bigham put in, unthoughtfully heightening everyone's apprehension.

Pointing to him, I whispered to Harold, "If we have a flat we won't need a jack 'cause Mr. Bigham can lift the car all by himself."

But more worry loomed on the horizon. We viewed it warily. Off to the south and southwest a bank of dark clouds hovered lowly over the earth, angry and sinister, poised to give birth to that dreaded whip tail twister so capable of wreaking devastation to anything in its path. Nothing happened however and in time, as if in accord with some remote signal, the clouds tore apart and fragment by fragment blithely disappeared into the air. The rest of the day stayed fair and clear.

"You ever see a twister John?" asked Mr. Bigham.

"Yep, sure have. Two, as I think about it. But at a distance."

"Well, I saw one once. Close up. I was in it."

"Is that so?"

"Yep. I was working the oil fields down around Olney, Texas. Had a good job rough necking, doing morning tower. Hey boys, in case you're listening, that means the midnight shift. I got Saturday off and went downtown. It was cloudy but I paid no attention. Nobody did. All at once, boom! Dust flying as thick as mud cause it was mud and raining cats and dogs all at the same time. Things whirling all around. Mud splattering all over my face. When it started gittin dark I knew I'd better head for cover, but didn't see any. So, I did the best I could. I laid down right then and there on the concrete flat on my belly next to a curb. I tried to dig holes into the concrete, I think. I know I tried to hold to the curb, but how do you do that? The next thing I knew that sucker picked me up 'bout six inches off ground level and bounced me like you would a rubber ball. Faster than you can bounce a rubber ball. With something like jackhammer speed. I thought it might shake out my teeth. Then just as suddenly as it picked me up it took a notion to set me back down. And as suddenly as it barged in on us it went away."

"Whew," my father half whistled. "You had one heck of a close call."

"You got that right. After turning over in my head what had happened I started opening that Good Book a heap more often. Talk about being spared. For what, I don't know. But I believe He spared me. "

During the course of his story I laughed not once, nor did I interrupt. It was scary.

While by and large we youngsters in the backseat enjoyed ourselves, there were nonetheless bouts of irritation. Brady gouged Harold in the ribs with his elbow, yapping "Move over, I'm scrouged," and if Brady failed to complain, then I became the culprit. Poor Harold! What a price the oldest son sometimes has to pay. Valiantly seeking to keep the peace he volunteered to sit between us, a position that he surely regretted but braced himself to accept it and stick it out. No finer brother ever lived I often told myself, and had to have the patience of Job to absorb with a minimum of complaint the unfair jostling dished out by his younger siblings.

When our travel covered a good sixty miles or more, I judge, my father decided that we all needed a much delayed respite and pulled over. "Surprise boys!" Before picking us up at the orphanage he stopped to see Grandma Wycliffe, who owned a farm east of Guymon. Through her persuasion my father made up his mind to place us in the orphanage when there seemed to be no reasonable alternative.

"We sure wish we could have seen Grandma Wycliffe too daddy," said Harold dejectedly.

"I know son, but I just didn't have time to take you," came a disappointed reply, not saying anything more of the matter, his pensive face suggesting perhaps at the moment that the journey ahead largely drew his contemplation.

Grandma Wycliffe lovingly sent along her blessings, a basket of fried chicken and biscuits, two Dixie Queen watermelons, and a gallon of iced tea, which not long into the trip turned from cold to warm but that made no difference. We would drink it and like it. "Let's eat," my father said brightly as he opened the basket of fried chicken while taking care not to let the Dixie Queens roll off the table. Brady whooped, "Wow, Dixie Queens," and did an up and down jig. We ate voraciously. I can still taste the chicken and biscuits.

My father and mother once lived for a brief while with Grandma Wycliffe on her farm not a lengthy distance from where he grew up. In fact, the farm belonging to his parents, a small unproductive parcel, abutted that of hers. I hazard to guess their homes set apart by two or three miles. The families were neighbors, yet he once said that he and my mother weren't acquainted until he returned from a two year stint in the military. They met at a Saturday night square dance in Guymon, a gala affair buttressed with cake walks and door prizes and watermelon cuttings. To gain relief from the grind of the past week the folks from the countryside near and far swarmed to indulge in the festivity. Deep into the wee hours the "whoopees" and "do-si-dos" resounded across the plains. With no substantial delay the acquaintance of the two youngsters waxed into love, and love soon into marriage. Once when rummaging through an aging trunk my eyes fell upon a fading yellow parchment that carried these words: "John B. Devine and Gladys Marie Wycliffe married on this date, March 1, 1920."

With the first baby approaching, and without sufficient means for supporting a family, he quit farming and set his sights on joining a wheat harvesting crew working back and forth across Kansas and Oklahoma. The wheat owners paid well, an incentive that drove him to stick it out until the season ended. Ironically it ended in Aurora, where my father and mother were renting, where she joined him just a few days before. There, they were to own their first home. My father and mother met with no difficulty in adjudging that farming did not seem so bad after all.

"Working the wheat fields. Ummph,ummph,ummph. Enough to kill a horse much less a man," he guffed, exasperation spreading over his face. "Moving, moving, moving. Always on the go. There's got to be something better."

"I know dear. You're right. Let's go back to what we know best."

Within the week they negotiated for a tired, eroding, desolate piece of soil called a farm glaringly absent of nutrients for producing even a minimal growth of crops, yet, unaware of what they were getting into delighted at the idea of calling it theirs. I once heard my father refer to the transaction as the worst doing of his entire life.

After another fifty miles or more we stopped for fuel, the filling station fronted with a huge yellow pump equidistant between two stucco textured columns upholding the pavilion. Ugly black dirt lay in front of the small little shack of a building, as well as under the pavilion, which the owners periodically treated with waste oil so as to settle the dust and transform the surface into a harder substance.

As we were pulling in Brady excitedly let out, " Hey, there's Shell Oil."

"That's right, they sell the gas," said father. "Shell's a good company. They drill oil wells south and east of here, further on around Enid, Alva, and Ponca City. Blackwell and Bartlesville too."

Outfitted in striped overalls and a railroad engineer's cap an emaciated figure hobbled from the doorway headed toward the gas pumps.

"Yon't me to fill er up?" he rasped, frowning at my father.

"Fine. Go ahead."

Still he hesitated. "Only thang I got is ethyl. That do?"

"That's fine. Go ahead. We're about empty. We'll take what we can get."

While pumping the gas the old fellow lifted his foot onto the bumper and kind of bent over, at the same time beginning to eye us boys uncomfortably crimped together, staring piercingly at one then another.

"What's he looking at?" Brady broke in.

It was our hair that attracted his fancy, wildly shaped, tousled and as entangled as spaghetti owing to the wind, not once feeling brush or comb since we left Guymon. No wonder.

"You boys look a sight, zactly like mop heads, zactly like mop heads." We said nothing, feeling a slight uneasy. My father and Mr. Bigham were around back doing a job. The old man kept jabbering, supposedly in regard to us, then — .

"Tell you what boys. You look wind whipped to me. Go on inside there and git yourselves some ice out of that cold drink box and put it in them fruit jars I see you got there with you. It'll help cool off your whistles."

As hard and crude as the old man appeared we knew then that it belied the truth, that in his soul there was couched a hidden caring generosity, and springing as young deer from the back seat onto the driveway we raced to the ice box. By the time we'd filled our fruit jars there sounded a beep, beep, beep, coming from the outside, the signal that father wished anxiously to start moving. With fruit jars in hand we dashed for the car and scrambled into the backseat.

Before we pulled away he turned to us. "What should you boys say?" he asked, tilting his head toward the old gentleman who stood close by.

"Thank you," we all said in staggered order, waving, the old man infirmly waving back as if to say good luck. My compassion overflowed. "What a lonesome solitary figure way out here on the plains. I hope he has someone who loves him."

Revived, we were back on the road moving at a thrilling rate of forty miles an hour, top speed for an older vehicle, even on hardtop surface. On dirt or gravel roads the rate would have been markedly slower.

From the start I had with penetrating keenness scanned the scenery and animal life along the way, but with the evolving change in the landscape my vigilance took on renewed vigor. I would begin to try to drink in more and more scenes, more than I could possibly digest, of the terrain and the sky above us, starting with the cradling hills encircling the lambent green meadows, a far cry from the flat barren plains two hundred fifty miles behind us where the land lay dry and dusty and ugly, the vegetation stingily restricted, where now and then you'd catch the lonesome ghostly silhouette of a range home, monstrous, made of heavy red stone hauled in from the Salado Quarry. It would have appeared on a distant but infrequent rise, the residence of the overlord or range boss who lived there with his wife and brood, a near duplicate of the description Mr. Bigham supplied of the Wagner ranch home in West Texas. He said he once worked for the Wagners. Not withstanding, a continuance of white boiling clouds rolled across the heavens and I imagined them as so many floating balloons. "I should do this more often" I advised myself. "Seldom does anyone take time to enjoy the beauty of these awesome creations, and after all the Master lives up there somewhere." Still, there were the other allurements — the zig zag flight of the haughty crow, trailed doggedly by an angered and determined sparrow, and two little antelope darting in and out of the nearby tree line, and brand new automobiles of variegated colors swooshing by at astonishing speeds in either direction. The obvious massive wheat fields swayed in the distance, drawing a patriotic comment from my father and reminding me of our national song. I spoke with amplified loudness.

"They say something in *America the Beautiful* about amber waves of grain."

"That's right son. You have a good memory. I'm proud of you. It's a great patriotic song. Every American should learn the words and sing it."

Knowing I sang the song times innumerable in chapel, sure of every line as well as the back of my hand, Harold and Brady cut their eyes at one another mischievously, on the verge of laughter at their younger brother's contrivance to draw notice from his daddy, yet I was the youngest, and so if I aspired to gain singular praise they wouldn't betray me.

We kept going, one hour after another. "How far have we come?" I wondered aloud. "How far is Guymon from here?" Though I declined not to speak of it my body seemed tired to the bone.

"It's way back there son, way back there," explained Mr. Bigham.

After a length I turned to something else which for sometime itched with a restlessness to surface, which during the excitement of leaving I temporarily pushed into sub consciousness. Our father had gotten a job, a good job, or so Brady said. "Good job," I recalled. Well hardly, though a gigantic improvement over his previous lot. Even so the work that he did drained a man and by some standards the company paid shamefully low wages. Driven by the boom, the State of Kansas started soliciting bids for building the highways and bridges north, south, east and west within its borders and Koss Construction Company headquartered in Topeka sought and received a handsome contract for administering the project, or some sizeable portion of it. Aggressive and smart, Koss was perhaps expected by anyone in the know to emerge with the award. My father heard of the firm and its ambitious undertaking, at once filling out an application for work handed to him by a church affiliated friend who already occupied a fairly high up position with Koss and mailed it to the director of personnel. To his astonishment he got hired to supervise a small road crew, a contingent made up of Mexicans and red neck cowboys, the notation of his military service appearing on his application a likely reason he ended up with the job. He would stay with the firm for the remainder of his work life, although in time the company promoted him to assignments of much greater satisfaction and responsibility that paid many steps above his starting rate. With the passing of another decade the nation plunged into the construction of a network of connected roadways, the interstates, stretching the full length of its borders, from ocean to ocean, from the Great Lakes to the Gulf, and Koss would enjoy even greater prosperity. No crystal ball would have been transparent enough to reveal that one day I would travel with my children to the great rocky mountains across the same highway that my father helped build.

We stopped sparingly to rest, to add fuel, and to check the tires, the latter worrying my father terribly as well as Mr. Bigham. Murmurs of concern arose frequently, but our luck held, and we crossed into Kansas without incident, fate smiling upon us for the continuation of the trip.

"How much longer?" I weakly asked as I saw the sign come shooting at us: Leaving Oklahoma, Entering Kansas. Whirling, I glanced backward at the whitish blur moving rapidly away, already becoming infinitely smaller.

"Not too long Tommy. Not very much further." We were at least two hours from Emporia. My father tried to be assuring, knowing though that we were worn thin and that his words likely would go for naught, and gestured to his front seat companion as if to say: Tell some funny stories, maybe that will help, and Mr. Bigham commenced; though faintly heard, his efforts lost by and large on unlistening ears, the three of us beginning to drift off to sleep, my head flopping on Harold's shoulder. Dark had overtaken us some time before. From the front Mr. Bigham reeled of a stream of endless assorted chatter, by now only talking to my father, frequently dwelling on personal experiences long past, sometimes switching to other subjects of currency and often threw in for good measure: "Whadda you think John?" The question was merely tacked on so as to stimulate my father's wakefulness who sat at the wheel. Every once in a while his voice faintly pressed through and I tried to erect myself. I loved listening to his tales, yet, more asleep than not, I hardly retained anything at all. The difficulty worsened from the torrent of the wind whipping across and around my ears. Finally, I gave up and sank once again into slumber.

The next day I wrote on the back of an envelope, a substitute diary sheet, fantasizing the courage and determination of our old jalopy at that intermission of the trip, especially when we were so close to our destination, as if I were personifying a grand steed of sort who now strove with every sinew within him to win the race. "Brave Heart plowed faithfully onward, grittily determined to finish the challenge, a gallant steed, perennial and immortal, throwing every ounce into the last surge, gasping, fighting, even convulsing, showing not one inkling of fading or giving up. It had come so very far. Brave Heart deserved a medal. Miles and miles lay behind us."

During my next return to consciousness the coarse elevated cry of Mr. Bigham rang out. "There it is. Old Emporia."

Awakened, we boys sat straight up, our necks straining like that of baby birds seeking a worm from their mother's beak.

"Where? Where is it?"

"There. See the lights. See." Mr. Bigham alternated to us in the back seat while turning back the other way to point to a glimmering of crystals five miles away, he said, and for every mile down to the very last we watched with dazzled eyes. At last the yellow sign with huge white letters evinced that we'd reached the city limits.

My father drove briefly hither and yon, steering left and right until coming to a fading stucco flat of Spanish vintage where he slowly brought the car to a halt so as to let out our friend. As an after thought he spoke warmly, "Tell Angelina we'll take her up on that enchilada supper real soon."

"I'll tell her John." Before Mr. Bigham had taken two steps he stopped. "Whoa! Goodnight boys. Sure been my pleasure." Then he walked away. I would never forget him. He had strengthened me.

Wearing a colorful flowery robe that clung loosely on her frame a pretty Mexican woman with nice dark hair falling about her shoulders stood in the doorway waiting. "*Bienvenido a casa mi marido.*" I did not speak Spanish but to me her words were sweet and warm.

Father drove us a few blocks further. "We must be near. Where is our house?" The car suddenly stopped. We were there.

"They're here, they're here," a woman of thirty or more shouted, a low subdued shriek that rippled with joy. It had to be Dollie, a lovely lady of medium height, blessed with an angelic smile and eyes so soft and captivating they could melt you. With golden hair flying in the wind she dashed across the yard to the car, giving no heed to the length of her dress that dragged the ground. I feared she might trip. Adoringly she wrapped her arms around our father, hugging and kissing him hungrily, then quickly turned to my brothers and me. She kissed our cheeks and hugged us lovingly, saving me for last, and letting us go for a slight backed away, looking us over absorbingly. I thought to myself, "How beautiful, how beautiful a woman. How lucky my father." The kindness that shone in her face spoke as a book of poetry. At once I knew we would all love her.

"Oh! Here are the rest!" Dollie's arms reached toward my brothers and sisters who raced from the front porch down the steps and into the yard where we were standing. They insisted on her coming first. I gaped at the family I had not seen in years. They were as strangers, barely recognizable. I learned a short while later that Rhonda and Gary were married, Rhonda two years before and Gary only recently.

"Harold, Brady, Tommy," they practically yelled, wild with joy, everyone shouting and trying to hug someone at the same time, out of control with happiness. Tears rolled down our cheeks. The clock hand at this hour struck eleven thirty, the commotion drawing the neighbors to their doorways, stretching their necks, but uncomplaining. They knew already that relatives were expected and likely to arrive late.

No one appeared to have noticed that a soft misty rain had begun to fall. Shortly Dollie took charge. "This is wonderful but we've got to go in. It's raining. Besides, I have food for you, lots of food," she announced, moving over at that instant to squeeze my arm. "You hungry Tommy? I can tell you are." She cupped my cheeks with her hands.

"I'm starved. My insides are growling." She grinned with twinkling eyes, as if to assure that she understood exactly.

"Well, guess what you all. We have chicken fried steak, tasty sweet milk gravy, and you can expect good hot biscuits in a jiffy from the oven. And there are loads of vegetables."

We stuffed ourselves with unforgivable portions, while Rhonda circled the kitchen hugging and kissing everyone. "I'm so happy," she cried. "At last we're together again."

The Coo of the Dove

IT WAS a long story, a struggle, but I'd gotten there, gotten admitted, gotten enrolled, and stuck it out. I'd gone to college at the University of Chicago and successfully completed two and a half years of academic studies, in addition to holding down a part time job which called for me to catch a plane each Friday and deliver legal documents to New York City. My sights were set on the university beginning when as a mere boy of seven my father and John Eric, my uncle from my mother's side, let me go with them on a trip to Chicago hauling a pick up truck load of green tomatoes they'd sell on the street. Even at that youthful age I gazed with astonishment at the magnificent edifices proudly cropping into view as we passed by the campus, my eyes incisively darting from one to another of these man made monuments.

"What's that?"

"The University of Chicago, it said back there on the sign," answered John Eric.

From that moment on that prestigious institution began to live inspiringly in my heart and in my youthful vision, and in the oncoming years I became increasingly determined to seek a share of the wisdom that coursed through the interior of its lordly walls. A boy of relative poorness I wasn't certain how I would get it done; but I found a way.

A mere few days remained before my third Christmas at the university and my thoughts were set on going home. I drove nearly four hundred miles to the outskirts of the small southern town of my birth. The proud fierce sun had begun to hide, streaks of red and gold the only observable fragments of daylight remaining. Darkness would soon follow, which descended early in the midst of winter. A current of warmth surged through my breast as I crossed through my mother's doorway. Glowing with happiness she gathered me into her arms, hugging me and taking on with tender loving endearments as if she would never let go. For a fleeting second I was once again her little boy and it had to be in her heart that she wished in fantasy that it could be so.

She cooked for a whole week in preparation, my oldest sister helping her, already there when I arrived and hugged me and took on over me as much as my mother. I had no more than settled into a chair when my mother asked for a report on things with me, starting with the last date of my coming to see her. She confused my academic studies with my part time employment at the law firm, the fault of her mix up altogether mine; for I failed to be painstaking enough in my letters to clearly set them apart.

"Tell me all about what you've been doing son. Especially in your law work."

"I'm doing all right mother. I deliver documents by plane from Chicago to New York, and this is coupled with my working for an older gentleman who keeps me busy researching things for him. Looking up things on paper."

"That sounds important. It really does. But could you tell me a little more so I'll better understand?"

"There's not much to it. I just dig into the files for information, legal stuff, concerning cases of law already tried and recorded. My job is to find out what actually happened and turn it over to Mr. Yazstremski."

"And who is that?" she asked, wrinkles gathering on her forehead.

"My boss. An older man. A fine man indeed. You'd like him. I study under him. I'm learning. I'm not a lawyer mom. I'm merely learning."

"But you will take up law someday, won't you?"

"I'm not exactly sure. I'm filling up with experiences and all sorts of legal knowledge but I'm not convinced at this stage that I'll venture into law as a life time profession."

"What will you do Ramsey? Have you considered another choice?"

"I have mom. I continually run it through my mind."

"What do you think it is?"

"Literature. Possibly literature."

"You'd like to be a teacher?"

"I would. I would in college. The idea is strongly appealing."

"A teacher. That's an awfully good profession."

"I feel it is."

It was a joyful Christmas. We largely ate. And stayed close to one another, laughing, talking, reminiscing, especially reminiscing which we did far more than focusing on the present or speculating on the future. Retreating to old times singularly swayed us. It was what families did back then. There were gift exchanges, but limited. My brother and three sisters were there, the two that were married having brought their children with them, hyper children, frenetically bouncing around everywhere, squealing, giggling, running wildly through the house. "I can't find it anywhere in reasonable belief that I'm an uncle," I silently confessed to myself. "It makes me feel suddenly old and the noise, the noise in particular, arouses a tinge of irritability." My youngest sister was yet unmarried, in the coming weeks planning to enroll at a nearby church supported college. The temptation came easily to me to compare our relative quietness, when the children were outside playing, to the spirited pre Christmas festivity at the university fraternity house where students gathered to celebrate the holidays before leaving for home.

The next day my mother relayed that John Eric, her youngest brother, dropped by during the week past with word that he needed to hear from me when I made it home, or as soon as I could follow through.

"What does he want? Did he tell you?"

"He's hopeful you can go with him and Sanford to the Harts Mill Bottom." Uncle Sanford was a brother to John Eric and my mother, older than John Eric by almost fifteen years. We thought of him as the hunter supreme. The Harts Mill Bottom was a swampy marshland inundated with flood waters in the spring by a slow crawling river without adequate embankment. When the flooding ceased the waters drained away and eventually disappeared in the muddy swirls of the Mississippi.

"When?"

"Let me look at the calendar. I wrote it down." She looked and gave me the day and date. But not the hour of departure.

"What time are we to leave?"

She looked once more at the calendar. "It says here five."

"Gracious! What an hour! I'll never lift myself out of bed that early."

"Oh you can. He's so hopeful you'll go with them. I think they've kind of planned it for you. Telephone him tonight that you'll be there at his house and on time."

After groaning in mild protest I concurred and picked up the phone and called John Eric that I wasn't about to resist joining a hunt that I knew would be tremendous fun. In no few words he went over the arrangements. We'd leave day after the next. We'd go in the wagon, hauling the dogs with us and the guns and some axes and a cross cut saw. Aunt Jewel, Uncle Sanford's wife, consented to pack food, foremost among it uncooked country ham and John Eric wove in that he was taking his oversized out of doors coffee pot and deep well frying skillets. He kept talking until I began to wonder if he ever might come to a stopping place. When he began to throttle down I lunged in and assured him once again that I'd be there and with great deliberation to say it politely bade him good night.

"Goodnight," he replied with a pleased thrill in his voice.

Uncle Sanford from his youth onward earned the reputation as a renegade in our family, not given to holding down a work for wages job and neither did he succeed in the productivity of farming. Sometimes he worked for short spurts at the cotton gin. His wife, a seamstress at a shirt factory kept his head above water, food on the table, that is. Not terribly bothered by over weightedness he suffered still from another handicap of worse potential, a hernia, an aggravation the doctors refused to correct with surgery, electing to treat it by wrapping an elastic strap around the lower contour of his stomach and around his testicles. It can't be said whether the strapping or the hernia itself, or both, should be singled out as the cause of his bending a slight forward when he walked, with a frown or a vagueness of pain visiting his face as if in haste to relieve a biological urge.

Of the seven days of the week Uncle Sanford spent three of them hunting rabbits with his beagles and on as many nights let loose his fox hounds over the same terrain. He quartered the fox hounds in separate kennels from the beagles under his front porch. Sometimes he stayed out for the greater portion of the night, the fox hounds on some fresh scent in hot pursuit, though never bringing their quarry to bay. That wasn't the point with Uncle Sanford. His whole delight centered on hearing the dogs whine and bellow as they poured tenaciously over the scented trail. Of the two leaders there was a distinct variance in soundings, a deep mournful bellow coming from Ned, the male, and a high abject whine lifting from Betsy the female. You'd hear Uncle Sanford calling out in the wee hours, yeow, yeow, yeow, as if he were honing in on the exact whereabouts of his prize trackers somewhere in the low soggy breaks. Sometimes he'd tilt his face toward one or the other of his shoulders, while cupping his hand to his ear, which gave the impression of his keeping pace with the entire pack foot by foot. In my growing up years I avidly looked forward to tagging along with him, staying by his side on many a night until twelve. By then, having stood for long uncomfortable stretches in the marshes, fighting against the cold, I'd return to the wagon long before he quit, and there, cover up with blankets and fall off to sleep. When the chase ended Uncle Sanford returned and to be sure that I got sufficiently awakened before starting home gouged his stiff fingers into my back.

"Wake up Ramsey. Time we went home. I need a riding buddy who's alert to help me make it back."

Likened to the winters past we left Uncle Sanford's that morning at slightly past five, the shadows of darkness stubbornly refusing to lift and disappear, the wagon bouncing unrelentingly against the convoluted surface of the dirt road, with the mules moving faster than their usual gait which I supposed they did to off set the coldness of the air. A foggy mist gushed from their nostrils as they breathed out. We could have taken John Eric's pick up for the transport of everything, the dogs, the camping equipment, the guns, and the rest and would have except beginning at a certain shift in the landscape the road gave out and from there on the terrain lay submerged in thickets and sedge and sloughs of backwater that good judgment advised against trying to cross, dangerous to undertake because of the entanglement of growth concealing swamp holes deep enough to swallow half of an automobile. An alternative therefore had to be sought for circling around these impediments. John Eric uttered lowly to himself that he'd decided wisely by not attempting to travel this way by truck. Uncle Sanford agreed. without speaking a word. His face said it all. No motor powered vehicle with wheels could have dealt with obstacles of this likeness, insurmountable and impenetrable, and with no other options conceivably available John Eric redirected the mules, thus altering our route and losing time. Uncle Sanford kept getting up from his driver's seat and when sitting back down collapsed his legs and sort of free fell to the wagon floor on his posteriori. The driver's seat consisted of a hard flat board with no backing against which to lean and no springs mounted underneath to counter the jolting impacts caused by the wheels bouncing up and down on the rugged surface of the road. Finally, after we'd covered a quarter of our journey I opened the coffee thermos that Aunt Jewel packed with the other provisions and drew the blankets up under my chin. Pouring a cup full I began to sip. On looking up I saw my two uncles smiling at one another — apparently at my antics of trying to get comfortable in the biting cold — gladdened that their young nephew was with them on the kind of adventure which in their spheres of reasoning made life worth living. I pulled the blankets up tighter under my chin, propped my shoulders against the siding, and got ready to endure the rest of the mileage, while my older kin folks unaffectedly braved the penetrating chill of the early day and at the same time carried on an unbroken stream of jibber and laughter.

We unloaded the wagon by early midmorning, ready, I thought, to turn the beagle hounds loose that yapped and whined and reared up on Uncle

Sanford's legs, impatient of waiting longer to start tracking a fresh scent. Their master wouldn't turn them loose just yet. "One thing about this weather," he pitched in. "It makes a man as hungry as a wolf. Gittin it ready are ye?" he kind of asked, kind of said, glancing over at John Eric Already John Eric kindled a fire, moving quickly in the cold to fry and serve a batch of ham and eggs before the hunt began, disregarding the beagles that whimpered and begged Uncle Sanford to let them loose. When the smell of coffee rose to my nostrils I got up and poured a cup full and sat back down. In no time I got up again filling my plate with ham and eggs I'd watched simmering in the cast iron skillet, which I could taste even before either entered my mouth. The out of doors atmosphere and the freezing temperature subtly combined to produce a voracious hunger, making every bite tastier, and I easily grasped what Uncle Sanford meant by his allusion to the weather provoking him, or any living man, to be as hungry as a wolf. I didn't tell my uncles that to me this was the highlight of the trip.

"Good, ain't it," Uncle Sanford let go, speaking to me from where he sat on the ground busily chewing a mouth full of biscuits and ham and eggs.

"Unh. hunh."

At last he called out, "Well, John Eric, it's time we turned them babies loose." The immortal hunt suddenly erupted and the immortal prey was soon in flight as the hounds leapt to the chase with a baleful cry. Our tactic focused not on staying up with the dogs, but rather to stand for awhile in one spot until they forced the rabbit from the underbrush, then move about sparingly, edging closer to an opening, which consisted of no better than briar infested swampy mush where we thought it might dart into view. The beagles did the moving for us, relentlessly in pursuit, the rabbit angling in a circular fashion until coming within range of the double barrel shot guns which required but one blast. The dogs instinctively fought through the spongy bog to retrieve the kill, the leader clutching it between gritty determined jaws until dropping it at the shooter's feet. This phase of the hunt was the fun part, the easy part, together with the stories told by my Uncle Sanford and John Eric of their growing up days as youngsters, some stretched beyond believable truth which they knew and knew that I knew. Their favorite tale referenced a panther of monstrous size and savagery that once roamed these marshes, sweeping up under cover of darkness and at will rifling corn cribs and dragging away half grown calves from the barn, never caught or stopped.

"Did they ever see him?"

"Now and then."

"But he wasn't ever caught or killed?"

"Naw. They found him one day though. He'd died of old age."

The hard part resulted from the fierce biting temperature, below freezing, to me colder than it actually registered on the thermometer, this because my hide wasn't lately accustomed to the out of doors. The bitter wind unhindered and unabated shot straight up the river and onto the adjoining naked shoreline, rich alluvial soil, which once grew tall and stately gum, hickory, ash, elm, cypress, and oak, affording an inexhaustible nursery of timber, whose roots grew deep into the unsunned earth that stayed damp and soggy from mid spring until mid fall. Now, this same soil harbored a sorrowful graveyard of dead and decaying stumps and logs.

"What killed the trees Uncle Sanford?"

"Pesticide. That's the way of them jerks over in the agriculture office. Caint leave well enough alone. Want to spray everything in sight. Bastards. I remember when nothing but big tall white oaks growed on the banks of this river as far as you could see."

I doubted his correctness of blaming pesticide for the fate of the trees, but I wasn't sure. Ecologists weren't sure themselves. I allowed it reasonable that Uncle Sanford's speculation equaled in accuracy the opinions or supposed facts rendered by the experts.

The effects of the icy water worsened by the hour, and even though I wore hip boots measuring to my lower waist the chill still penetrated to my legs. In time, it begun to creep through the walls of the boots and into my skin, the discomfort eventually driving me to leave the hunt for solid ground where the wagon and mules were left and where John Eric pitched on the fire a couple of gnarled looking stumps which put it to burning brightly just before we set out. Seeing it reduced to an ember I punched it up and piled chunks of wood on the ashes that covered the stubborn dying coals still holding on, with the result that very quickly small finger size flickers converted into knee high flames; and then I dropped down on a log close by and extended my half numb sockless feet into the radiant warmth. With the noon hour nearly passed, Uncle Sanford and John Eric came dragging back from the marshes with a string of rabbits tied to their belts, the dogs drenched and muddy with hassling tongues hanging out one side of their mouths faithfully trailing.

"Let's eat Ramsey. You hungry?"

"Famished." Then, eyeing the pile of game they'd thrown to the ground I curiously asked how many we'd killed so far.

"Twenty four."

"Ha. A bonanza."

To my mind we couldn't have done better. I could only be credited with four of the twenty four but felt fully satisfied. I'd come for the thrill of the trip more than for the limited count of game that I bagged.

Then came the skinning and the messy evisceration, the gutting of entrails, of at least three rabbits, already starting to stiffen. John Eric proceeded through these steps with admirable exactness and rapidity, his skilled hands taking him through the same steps hundreds of times before, beginning when but a youthful boy. He could have waltzed through these exercises in his sleep. I could have done the same. I'd also undergone years of practice, not as many but a good many, and this he knew. He in part trained me. I offered to help. He declined: "I'll be through here in a jiffy. You can do it next time." So I merely looked on. When he finished he threw the entrails to the beagles, then dipped the raw carcass into a container of salty brine, churning it up and down until the least tint of blood was altogether washed away, and then there followed the briefer chore of rinsing. Then he sliced the meat into multiple pieces, the size of each as big as a chicken thigh and dropped them into a skillet of hot grease, or lard, there resulting a staccato of crackling, an intense popping or fizz, and John Eric, in an effort to avoid the dangerous splatter jumped back, using his arms and hands to shield his face. Uncle Sanford fidgeted and fumbled with starting the coffee to brew, not in a modern streamlined percolator with a transparent dome but in John Eric's oversized coffee pot, in actuality a heavy cast iron container, into which without measuring, merely guessing the right amount, he poured a ground up quantity of coffee beans. Strong and boiling hot the coffee would taste good. It always tasted good in the open air. John Eric had timed setting the biscuits on the fire so they would bake and be done when the rabbit meat finished frying or thereabouts.

"Okay Sanford, you and Ramsey fill up them plates and pour your coffee. It's time we got after it."

We were ravenously hungry. Me, more than my uncles. My stomach started to growl an hour before. We found a place to sit close to the fire and for the longest unforgivably stuffed ourselves with John Eric's cookings, which, I thought to myself tasted as good if not better than any I'd ever tasted and I said as much to him. And feeling it wise not to leave him out I complimented Uncle Sanford on his making the coffee. We rested for the better portion of an hour after we'd finished eating, the rabbit meat and biscuits already long gone, all the same to me, for I couldn't have ingested another bite but managed more coffee.

Uncle Sanford had stretched out on the ground not far from the fire with his head propped against a convenient log and appeared so peaceful that I suspected he might have fallen into a doze.

But all at once. "Ain't it quiet out here? The first of the week I came out here to run the dogs and got to listening to a dove coo over yonder. Now that's a sound for you. I just laid and listened for the longest like I sometimes do. I've always liked to hear that sound."

"A dove cooed Uncle Sanford? At this time of year?"

"Sure it did. I heard it. I know my sounds."

"Oh I know that. But the cold!"

"It was warmer then by a good bit, and besides, even if it had been cold a dove can find a place to keep warm, in a tree hole, under rocks, in old deserted barns, and stumps — shelters like that — and can come out a little bit at a time and go back in."

"I didn't know you listened to doves."

"I do. They're precious little creatures."

"But you used to shoot them in the fields after corn gathering. John Eric and I went with you."

"Not any more."

"Why'd you quit?"

"Well, I'm not good about going to church but I go sometimes. Jewel nags me that I should. I heard the pastor talk about the dove one Sunday; said a dove landed on Christ's shoulder when He got baptized, and that it more or less was the Lord, or something Holy to stand for the Lord. That's why I don't shoot doves anymore. And whenever I hear that sound, that lonely coo — there's not another bird sound on earth like it — it bears on me as something religious. As I say, the dove is a precious little creature, and it has to be because the Good Lord made it. The coo of the dove is special Ramsey."

It loomed in my contrivance. There was an aspect of the dove and the muddy devouring swamp and Uncle Sanford that seemed uncannily to tie them together, that since the beginning of infinity they existed as immemorial kinsman. "Of course the first two will go on and on, but not Uncle Sanford. One day he'll reach the climax and the Lord then will throw away the mould for sure and for good by which He made him, figuring that the replication of another hybrid of his likeness might be inadvisable because He won't see him fitting well into the complexity of a changing modern world. But he'll be needed. His kind always is."

The conversation seemed to have mysteriously cropped up. I couldn't have remotely expected it from my dear old uncle, ever. Even so, I nonetheless took it that I'd received a profoundly important message from a man with less than half the education that I possessed — but that stored within the environs of his wisdom there abided an experience and an understanding that put my learning in the shade.

I would that night, when I lay in bed, commence to revolve what he had said and failing after a time to succumb to slumber rose and opened the Scriptures for a certain passage which I'd read innumerably. I knew the story well, having read it many times more than the number of my fingers and toes, and even lots more — but urgency ran through me to read it again. "*As soon as Jesus was baptized, he went up out of the water. At that* moment *Heaven was opened and he saw the Spirit of God descending like a dove and alighting on him. A voice from Heaven said, 'This is my Son whom I love; with him I am well pleased.'"*

"Well fellas," Uncle Sanford let out, glancing at the sun nearing the mid afternoon angle in the western sky. "Let's get back to what we came for. The dogs are rarin to go again. And today the trail is hot . Rabbits as thick as hops. What do you say Ramsey?"

"Sure. Let's go."

I wasn't ready if the truth were known. Warm for the first time since early morning I would have voted to pack up and head home if the jurisdiction dwelt in my hands or for a while longer lie lazily around the warmth of the fire. Besides, the temperature now registered a slight lower with the wind picking up after a lull during the hour that we were eating. But, careful not to groan in his presence, I reluctantly forced myself up and pulled on my hip boots and we began the second phase of the hunt.

Rather than wade into the water again I spotted a stump not far from the periphery of the swamp and sat down with my gun across my lap, finally electing to get up however and reposition myself in a clearing nearer the river's edge. In the meanwhile Uncle Sanford and John Eric sloshed further down stream and picked an out of the way recluse for standing in wait until the prey came in sight. It was but a pittance until a rash of yelps from the beagles pierced the air fresh and vigorous, and abruptly, an explosion echoed loudly from the gun of one or the other of my uncles. Soon I learned which. Uncle Sanford yelled out, "I got im," and affectionately pampered Elsie, the she bitch, his favorite of the pack, for her efforts at retrieving the kill. Despite his age and infirm posture he still shot as well as the younger hunters who hunted with him and still killed as much of the game as he ever killed. For the next two hours, the sun descending faster than we liked, guns went off with unchecked regularity, though less than during the morning hunt, until at length Uncle Sanford called it quits. When coming into my vicinity he asked for the number I had taken down, "two," I said, and then he counted sixteen that we as a team killed since lunch, making forty all told for the entire outing. Moving about in the attitude of a rheumatoid sufferer he started to gather the guns and the iceless ice coolers while John Eric and I loaded the rest, the sleeping bags, the axes, the dogs, the blankets, and the previously gutted rabbits, and hitched the mules to the wagon and then we commenced our trip home. On the way back there was a decided hush in our bearing, each of us too tired to do much talking. I rode as before on the bedding of the wagon with the beagles, whereas John Eric held the reins to the mules, while leaning a kilter Uncle Sanford planted his right hand against the siding to keep from toppling over. He looked down at me and admitted what I saw in his tired and drooping face. "A full day Ramsey. I'm damn near worn out. I'm getting old."

I marveled at the ruggedness and determination of my two uncles, men of the soil, their spirit firmly planted in nature, perfectly cut to have joined the early pioneers of our country in quest of charting a path for future generations. It was warmly comforting to know their brand still dwelled among us. They were who they were but nothing more, not of the faintest inclination to be more, past, present or future, satisfied with the abilities and limitations the Lord allotted to them. Never could they have sat as chairman of a giant corporation, nor been a lettered minister of a big city church, nor a doctor of medicine and surgery, nor any of the budding young geniuses at the university that I knew — none of these — but they were significant in their own right, and as I deeper penetrated into who they actually were I began to wonder to what degree this nation might have stopped short of its present acclaim without men of this caliber, men of sturdy stock. While John Eric seldom let it come to surface and Uncle Sanford not at all, this I knew: they were proud in the extreme of the academic pursuits of their nephew and enveloped more than a vague notion of what it entailed. Back at the fraternity house my little group sometimes touched upon the lot that man had been consigned to occupy in his life on earth and why that came to be. Now, I began to address this complexity alone, using my uncles as the major sources of analogy. "Why," I asked, "is it that there is such a gaping imbalance between men, an imbalance that starts at birth? Are my uncles whom I hold dearly in my heart victims of a bad card that destiny has dealt them? Ah, but wait. Who has been dealt a bad card, you are they? Who is to say what a good or bad card is? Didn't you see how ecstatically they enjoyed themselves today? Drunk with elation and joy. It depends, doesn't it, on how you choose to look at things. To you, the pain and discomfort you suffered out there, or kind of that, amounted to a peak of joy to them. Neither Uncle Sanford nor John Eric would consider for a single minute trading places with you. Have you thought of that? It's true. You are of the same lineage as your uncles and you have always loved doing the things they do, but why did you turn out so much to the opposite? Is that not the strangest? Why is that so? Well, I guess it just is. Sorry. If you are determined to know, why don't you ask the Good Lord? He's the one up there who deals the cards."

When we reached Uncle Sanford's home he crawled stiffly down from the wagon and waved off our offer to help with the mules and the miscellany of transports he'd need to put away. He said goodnight and then thoughtfully came over and slapped my arm. "Good to have you out with us young buddy."

After we loaded the equipage in the truck that belonged to John Eric he drove us to his home where he let me out and then I crawled into my car and drove to my mother's home. Dark had fallen sometime earlier. She met me at the doorway.

"Did you make it okay?"

"Yeah. Very well." I tried to sound of good spirit. She smiled, though showing in her countenance that she knew I inflated my answer for her sake. "But I'm frozen stiff."

"Oh, my dear. I'll fix you some hot chocolate. That'll warm you up."

Hardly had I made a dent in my drink when she asked for a report on the hunt, chiefly if my part went well.

"I enjoyed it. By and large I did. But as I have intimated the cold bit into my skin with oppressive bitterness. On the other hand the food out in the open tasted salivatingly good, and the travel in the wagon to and from truly returned as a throwback to the days I often long for. I liked that a great deal. And the rabbit kill was soooooperior, far beyond what I expected. We got forty in all. I think that's right. But the highest on the pedestal had to do with the story I heard about the coo of the dove."

"The coo of the dove? What is meant by that?"

"Well, it's sort of hard to explain, so if you will mom wait and let Uncle Sanford tell you. He can do it so much better."

Anatole Wutherington

I LEARNED FIRST her name, Anatole Wutherington, the daughter of a famous entrepreneurial family, the victim of a kidnapping, these facts supplied to me by my grandmother with whom I had come to visit as we made our way along a well known boulevard of a large sprawling city on an oppressively cold day in January of the year 1915. She had lived there since drawing her first breath, the place also of my father's birth who upon the attainment of manhood married and moved to another state. I distinctly recall being with her because just as the century had acquired fifteen years of age so too had I, the same as the girl's age when she was abducted.

Strong and spirited my grandmother was a walker, equipped with the stamina to transcend a lengthy distance without pause or rest, and on this day we with good steady paces passed by one building after another — strange sights to my inexperienced eyes, old European vintages erected in the formative years of the city — finally coming to a stoppage where in the looming there stood a towering immense edifice that I recognized from having seen a near identical likeness in books and magazines, a Cathedral of Gothic Romanesque style, to which she alluded as a Catholic Church. She shifted slightly to face the structure, turning her back to the north while drawing her heavy woolen coat tighter around her person in the movement, which I assumed she did as an adjustment to counter the nippy winter air. It was not for the purpose of abating the chill that consumed her interest, not this at all; the whole of her concentration aimed only at gaining a more advantageous view which she had done by altering her angle of stance.

"That's where it happened," she uttered, dropping her voice to a lowness that interfered with my grasping clearly her words. The thought of it hurt her still.

"What? What did you say grandmother?"

"I said that is where it happened. The kidnapping of a young girl. The place where he held her."

"What girl? When? How?"

"Anatole Wutherington. A young beautiful girl. News of it spread like wild fire throughout the city. Her face appeared on the front page as constantly as a stream."

"When was this?"

"Five years ago. In the month of November. I recall it as if it were yesterday."

Then she began to tell the details of struggle that befell the young girl in her painful experience and it is this story that I now, after fifty years have expired, tell again from memory and copious notes with pen in hand setting it down on paper.

It was not in the main body of the church that the kidnapper kept her, not in the facade portion that one saw from the street, nor in any of the adjacent wings, but in the back corridor which for some time had been undergoing heavy construction, a sizeable erection of the framing and roofing finished. They said that it happened in early evening, when dusk had overspread the city, that he lunged from a car, stolen, no less, and dragged her into it and sped away, coming to the very grounds that my grandmother and I stood facing, from which, as yet in an unexplained feat, he pushed, carried, or forced her at weapon point to the upper height of the incomplete section, there both crawling across a narrow catwalk, a perilous thing to do, to an attic space where he would hold her in seclusion. Of shoulder height a guard rail stood affixed to the side of the catwalk for one to hold to while moving across. If it broke or otherwise gave way the user would almost certainly fall with it to the depths below, there if not landing on the hard crude earth directly then likely striking the heavy monstrous machinery idling in scattered patches throughout the storage yard or crashing onto the jagged stacks of wooden materials stored in the proximity of the machinery. In either event one could not fathom an ending other than instant death. It was not long forthcoming that Anatole, of remarkable agility, snappily took to moving across — she could have danced her way over, her captor, amazed at what he saw, but fearful of heights himself, continuing to crawl. The catwalk led directly into the attic space, which the assailant calculated beforehand to be a thoroughly unlikely recess for a workman or workmen of the church to come looking for something. Built of exceeding limitations it could accommodate but a small amount of form, two human beings and an assortment of minimal survival necessities. As soon as they entered she sank bewildered and in shock to the flooring, looking into nothingness, the dark, but found to her amazement a matting of some thickness on which she now partially sat — for not enough height existed to let her sit completely erect — certain of what it was for, for her, and a pillow at one end on which to rest her head. She then lay down with her back to her kidnapper, who seemed already asleep and with his back to hers, trying desperately to keep distance between them. He made no effort to edge closer, which she feared he might, but this did not occur, nor was there a semblance anywhere in his bearing to indicate a tendency to molest her. Even in her stressful if not frenzied state she somehow sensed and felt that he did not scheme to violate or otherwise harm her, although judging this not to be the norm of kidnappers, fearing that behind his keen piercing eyes there lurked a mind of derangement. She prayed silently that he would treat her humanely. After lying prostrate for some few hours, virtually unmoving, she began to deliberate her circumstances even more assiduously than she already had.

"This is unbearably restricting, even if he has untied my wrists. How terrible these cramps and the pain will only worsen as the night grows longer. Oh my Dear Lord. How can I bear this?"

He lay between her and the doorway but it rushed to her that she might suddenly push over and past him and before he awoke and caught on to the unanticipated commotion could on all fours scamper to the doorway and cross the catwalk, escaping down the stairs. Once in the open, she believed, she could outstrip him. But then recalled that on their way into the attic he locked the door behind them and kept the key.

Covers were sufficient in numbers and thickness to keep her warm as the night wore on, she judged, aware that in the late hours the temperature descended sharply, but this seemed a moderate worry; the worst of worries, besides what her captor might do to harm her, being the tightness of their quarters, so tight that — "I can't even stretch my legs much less sit up or get up and walk about. How will I endure this? How long will he keep me here? Oh God. We've just got here. Will it be days? Or months? What a terrible thing this is. Maybe it's not real. Maybe it's, it's — . But oh it is Anatole. You have to believe it." And then, thinking, thinking. "Sir.

Mister. Can I say something? Will you talk to me? Please." She now sat up as much as the ceiling allowed.

"Ummmm."

"Will you talk to me?"

"What do you want?"

"I'm awfully cramped. I suffer. My arms and legs hurt most painfully. Could we leave this place for awhile so that I can gain relief?"

"Not tonight."

"Not tonight! Oh! The night will be incredibly long. Then tomorrow?" No answer, not immediately, but after a bit.

"No. Not tomorrow. Tomorrow night. Yes."

The rest of the night and all day tomorrow, the thought ran through her, imagining how horrible the next several hours to follow, but concluding it to be of no use to plead further, and afraid if she did such might tick him off. Defeated, she sank back onto the matting. This night and the next day were the worst of the hours of her confinement, those that followed by degrees becoming somewhat less restricting and immeasurably less stressful, particularly after the first week. On the second night he obeyed his promise; they would leave the attic and spend the greater part of it on the lower interior of the church, almost until dawn. To do so was to have pity in his heart for the girl, it has to be supposed, and from a concern that to prolong her confining existence might damage both her mind and health.

The assailant skillfully undertook the crime with careful pre analysis of his hideaway and the making of arrangements for food, water, and clothing, clothing especially for the girl, and blankets and pillows and flashlights. Lighting of any consequence he cautiously refused to use, only candles that emitted a wee glow when he took it to be an absolute necessity and he brought in a dispensary on the first night, a metal container of use to the girl in relieving her biological processes. One has to assume that he attempted to consider and provide for everything, this taking into account the use of the kitchen and expansive dining room at night that occupied the full run of the basement floor of the main interior, which required the dangerous crossing of the catwalk, descending the steps three flights down, spanning the spacious courtyard garden, and with a turn or two entering the kitchen. These maneuvers he accomplished as easily and surely as he could in broad daylight, for during the passage of several months past he practiced them as an athlete might a callisthenic and even if he were encumbered with the presence of his hostage he regarded it as only a minor burden. He could guide her and stay unerringly on course. It was not that she hindered the accuracy of his movements that posed a bother but the handicap of quickly hurrying her out of sight once in the area of the kitchen should he detect that someone might be entering from the outside. Alone, he could dart away into the shadows and through the doorway, escaping detection; yet that advantage appeared now seriously impaired and he cautioned himself that he must keep a wary eye and ear. At first he kept her hands tied while leading her from the attic to the kitchen, then upon entry untying them without explanation, despite his wariness of an intruder, done perhaps due to the girl's pleading to remain free, that the cords hurt her badly, which began to weigh upon the tender places of his compassion.

Mass was held in the sanctuary on the upper floor from where they were, on mornings daily at eight, only at very limited intervals the kitchen and dining room put into use — usually when overflow gatherings were experienced with which her captor of faultless inborn stealth seemed to be versed with respect to date and hour, though fantastic this was. Over time he had been privy to unlimited storages of food, milk, and juices, and raw fruits, as well as operating the gas fed cook stove, and even learned by subtle feel whether his fingers were touching knife or fork or spoon, and could differentiate instantaneously the quality of glass ware, whether the raised ornament of the surface featured Roman or Grecian architectural origins. Insatiable was his yen for wine, and this he found in a secluded cupboard, which he appreciated directly from the flask, but more so when seated and sipping from the finery of a receptacle, which one has to believe he could not have known to be a Chalice that the good priests utilized in the ceremonious conduct of the Sacrament of the Eucharist. The wine he shared with the girl, almost kindly, "Here, take some; it's good," handing her an unopened flask, which she accepted and poured a glass half full, the instant alertness of her intellect telling her that the sweet substance so rich of nutrients might prove of value in maintaining her strength and vigor as she battled to endure her horror and somehow miraculously stay alive and escape. Now, and even after now, the officials of the church did not seriously catch on or believe that food stuffs and drink were getting lifted from the storages, only slightly suspecting they were, and that if the thefts truly were beginning to occur the disappearance resulted from their own maintenance force, among which were the cooks, and that the one or ones of singular guilt could not be easily ferreted out. Seeing more than ordinary importance in maintaining good will between themselves and the workers they were hesitant to instigate an investigation, and therefore took no action, merely sloughing off the nettlesome distraction as not a priori bother.

Until gaining confidence that no one might notice their presence from the outside his undertakings were exacted in darkness, though a faint glow of moonlight on most nights sifted stealthily through the limited narrow windows. She watched in a tad of disbelief as he zipped about in the dimness, wizardly lifting meats from the ice box and pans from the cabinets and canned produce from the pantry. At all times he commanded that she stay close at his side. Soon the meal was ready. Sitting at a side table, they ate, and when finishing walked for limited stretches, particularly back and forth to the dining area, the girl beseeching for continued exercise and persuaded him to allow her plea. And there was another imperative, the needed use of the toilet. At times in the attic she could not hold back and of necessity, unable to longer resist the force of nature, employed the metal container for elimination. While carried out in the dark the thought of his presence, even so close that she easily heard him breathe, weighed strenuously upon her. "This is eerie, insane, a nightmare."

But now, at last, they were in the kitchen and with aquiline vision she at once spotted the lettering above the doorway off to the opposite side of the room. "Please. Can I use the bathroom while we are down here?"

"Use it. As much as you need. I expect you to. We'll be here most of the night." His tone and manner were gentle, as if having a sentiment of caring in them.

"Most of the night. That sounds wonderful. And tomorrow? Will we — ?"

"We'll go back to the attic at daylight or a little before. We'll sleep tomorrow. All day."

So, with that she made her way to the toilet, to the women's facility, called the ladies room on the name plate. On entry she heard the lock snap as he closed the door, taking no chances of her escaping. Then she locked the door from the inside and after the eliminations hurriedly washed herself. Wash cloths were stored in shelves above the sink. "Oh what a relief. This feels so good. Seems like I haven't bathed in weeks." Gambling that no one would enter the kitchen during his absence he sometimes momentarily left the area for reasons that he did not disclose, apologizing for retying her hands and affixing the loose end of the bonds to a heavy steel column that stood near the center of the room, or, oddly, sometimes returned her to the women's toilet and locked the door, though not binding her. Aside from a few instances in the whereabouts of the kitchen the only other periods in which he bound and tied her resulted when he left her unguarded in the attic. In this he was to a degree peculiarly inconsistent, sometimes binding only her hands, leaving the rest of her extremities unsecured, and of this laxity she especially made mental notation. When there, which was for the most part, he passionately saw to it that she remained free.

Came the daylight, the horror and dread of the attic beginning all over.

"Must we go back now? Can't we stay a while longer?"

"No," he answered with an accent of gruffness, not harsh, but detectably irritable, which unexpectedly showed itself. She would not test him further, apprehensive of disturbing a side not yet seen, a dangerous side possibly.

While thus far he reflected a gentle nature and showed surprising kindness it would nevertheless not leave her that at the faintest provocation he might unravel. "Easy Anatole. You must go easy. In there somewhere there has to be a disturbed soul, two souls, one subdued and in control and another likened to a powder keg, a spark away from exploding. Do not cause a spark. Little by little win his confidence, keep him settled, and by so doing you'll gain more freedom and face less danger."

But let us return to the very first of her terrible ordeal and the unraveling of events in the hours and days following.

It was November, on an ordinary day, the temperature moderate and Thanksgiving close around the corner that the eruption took place. Anatole Wutherington left home on her customary walk, selecting a course she pursued times countless, attired in quite sporty regalia, a dark skirt and heavy red sweater, but a scrutiny of certain records — letters, dairies, news releases of 1910 — made no mention of other clothing that she wore on her person. Her hair, a lengthy gorgeous brown, lapped onto her shoulders. She walked at a lively pace, likened to that of my grandmother in her agile not yet aging years. Athletically inclined, she always walked lively, and few friends, or anyone, were with her because of the swiftness of her pace. When leaving that late afternoon she looked dapperly back over her shoulder and assured her mother that she'd not stay long, thirty or forty minutes, an hour at the most — returning before nightfall in any event. But she did not return in the range of time she'd given; she would not return at all, and soon, as the night closed in, the mother anxiously telephoned the father and then "all hell broke loose" as said by the Chief Magistrate when later meeting with a consortium of reporters. Suddenly, the whole city reverberated with alertness, policemen on horseback, on foot, and in cars darting excitedly to every place configurable in search of the girl's whereabouts, the start of a wild goose chase and a never ending and frenetic combing of the city in an effort to discover what happened to her.

There were no warnings, not the thinnest hint to anyone that she would abruptly disappear, all at once vanish, and despite the police's interrogations of the neighbors who lived along the street where Anatole chose to carry out her daily ritual, not one could shed light on anything helpful. So they kept at it. The first day's search turned into the second, the second into the third, the third into the fourth, the fourth into the fifth, the fifth into the sixth, the sixth into the seventh, and by sundown a full week was behind them, still no Anatole, still the police baffled, no closer to a discovery of the girl, some now beginning to wonder if they were up against a hideous complexity that extended beyond the reach of solution, and that there would never be a solution, given the fact that they were acting on no more than a starting point of when she left and where she left. After that, not the minutest clue.

"Search the buildings, search every building, certainly the ones on the back side of the city," the Chief Magistrate exhorted, his eyes flashing, "Drag the lakes, question the druggies, and the winos, put heat on the ex cons and the parolees, interrogate her friends, see into the recent youth parties which she might have gone to, sit again with the parents to learn more, something they might have overlooked; look into all these potentials. Spare no one. Spare no cost. The father will spend his last dime to get her back."

As could not be expected otherwise the mother fell to pieces, hundreds of imaginings rushing through her at once, couldn't sit down, couldn't rest, paced the floor, at times on the verge of screaming, and what mother would not have succumbed to such stresses so savagely tearing at her. She was a perfect mother they said, adoring of her beautiful daughter and that the daughter lovingly reciprocated her affection — two inseparable people, often seen on the streets walking hand in hand, in the happiest of temperament patronizing the boutiques together, and now terror had struck the mother's heart, who doubtless wondered if her daughter yet lived, and if she did what abuse, and possibly torture, was she going through. The family — the father, the mother, and Anatole — lived in a stylish Georgian home west of the city, comfortably decorated and furnished but not by any measure excessive, and though rich, electing to live like folks of the neighborhood, in fall and winter evenings simply sitting before an open fire immersed in one another. Her parents meant everything to her; they were her heart and soul. Sometimes folks heard her say fondly of them that they were two incredible rocks in her life. "An ideal family," the neighbors said and that in their view it would be unfathomable that any of the three were the object of enemies, further declaring it exceeded the bounds of normalcy that someone would have committed such a despicable act against them.

"It has to be a kidnapping," said the Chief Magistrate in a statement to the press. "It just has to be. There's nothing else to believe or suspect. It's money that's behind it. Naw, the girl didn't run away. I know her. She wouldn't have done that. And it's not vengeance that somebody's up to. It's a kidnapping for money and that's what we're going on. Any day now I'm looking to see a ransom note. It's coming. In the meanwhile we've damn well got to try to find her."

More than two weeks lay in the background and Anatole Wutherington had endured long dreadful hours in a state of captivity, during which she and her captor alternated between the attic and the kitchen vicinity of the church. She on the very start began to count the days of her confinement by the ingenuous deduction of tying a knot in the shoe lace she snitched from one of the pair of tennis shoes that her kidnapper confiscated for her. Necessity begets a strange magic which can make things of common routine usage become precious. As each day dawned afresh she tied a new knot, mindful of what day it was, Tuesday in this case, and counted the knots in succession as the days progressed, thereby knowing on any given moment the number of days of her captivity. In time her circumstances changed some for the better, in that her kidnapper with the aid of a flashlight created another space in the attic for her, accomplishing this by tearing away a raft of boards that formed part of the partition, sounding pleased when commenting that now with his work done she could stretch her legs and arms and sit up and do limited exercises. Wisely, she thanked him.

As she lay on her matting one day waiting for sleep to come she raised up a slight with her elbows, hearing a tremor of laughter on the street in front of the church she supposed, or was it traffic, heavier than usual, but when the commotion lessened and ceased she thought perhaps she was mistaken, and then disappointed again lay down and began to drift back to the beginning moments of her incredulous predicament. She often did. "He was of such crude appearance when he dragged me into the car, burly, unshaven, coarse of voice, shadowy. Ah, how awful my fear. I made no effort to speak. I knew I couldn't. But at last, in seconds I guess, I managed to pleadingly ask him not to hurt me. 'I won't hurt you,' he said in a very low voice. Now that I see him in candle light when we are in the kitchen he is much different, quite normal, looking just like anyone else, except for his eyes, narrow and piercing, and mean. But sometimes sort of gentle. But do not delude yourself Anatole. This person is not an ordinary drifter, or thief, or wonderer. Something is bad wrong with his mental faculties, or else he wouldn't have done this terrible unnatural thing. He's crazy, unbalanced, and could go off at any minute. Why did I not scream when he grabbed me that night? Shock I guess. It seems now that I should have. But I didn't. You never know what you'll do when something like that so horribly descends upon you. And why didn't I struggle to wrench myself free? The same answer again, yet not quite the same. His arms wrapped around me as if they were a vice of steel, closing with astonishing force, seeming as if they might crush me. What great strength! And when we climbed the stairs and got to the attic doorway another opportunity suddenly seemed of reach. While he gripped my arm and fumbled with the keys I could have shoved him and run across the catwalk and down the stairs and made good my escape. I didn't. Like lightning I calculated whether to do it or not, deciding that failing in my attempt was to invite my oblivion. So here I am. I must stay strong, must not cry or fall into despair. The greatest trial I face I think is to convince myself that some way, somehow I can and will endure any and all suffering that comes, until at last I'm free and safe at home. Maybe there's a way out of this. Maybe the Good Lord will answer my prayers. They're looking for me. I know they are. I know they are around the clock. I'm sure. Maybe they'll find me. Please hurry all of you and rescue me. Ah, my poor father and mother. Goodness! What are they going through? What thoughts can be surging through them? Just to hear their voice, even by phone, would be more than precious. Only a word. Or read a note from them. Or send them one myself."

Some few days expired beyond the third week when she began tallying the knots in the shoe lace, silently murmuring that right away she'd need to draw one from the other shoe. "Twenty five knots, twenty five days, and nothing. Nothing from the city police, or from anyone looking for me and nothing from him as to why he's keeping me here. I've got to start talking to him to find out. Pressing him is dangerous perhaps but why not run the risk. I'm just withering away as it is without raising a hand to help myself."

One night soon they sat at the side table having the supper meal and though he had not lit candles, and apparently chose against it, the moonlight shone through the windows with a glow of unexpected brightness, bright enough to allow both to see with ease one another's face. She spoke calmly but with a determined cast.

"I've not asked you yet. Don't you think I ought to have your name? How can I carry on a conversation with you unless I do?"

It seemed that he resolved to remain silent. She thought he might be all at once stupefied, caught with a question completely unexpected, for no presence came to the man's face in manner or movement to suggest he had now begun to turn it over. But suddenly he stuttered, then swoosh.

"Osgood Nesbitt. It's Osgood Nesbitt."

"Oh thank you. And mine as you know, I'm sure, is Anatole Wutherington."

"I know your name. I know it well. And I know you well too."

"How? Why?"

"At church. You go to the Lutheran Church, the big one on the west side of town."

"You've seen me there?"

"Umm, huh."

"Do you go to church there?"

"Yes and no. I dropped in once and saw you. I saw you in the choir. I've kept going back ever since. Only at times."

"How old was I when you first saw me?"

"Thirteen."

"You knew exactly."

"Yes."

"And you've tracked me ever since."

"Yes."

"Why?"

"I won't say."

"Okay. But tell me this. You owe it. Why are you keeping me like this?"

"The money."

"But have you sent word to my parents? To ask for the money? They'll give it to you then you can let me go. You won't have to let me off any place. You can just turn me loose. I can find my way back."

The angle of the moon suddenly shifted, the room fading into a dimmer glow, and as a consequence Anatole could not tell whether he deliberately dropped his head forward so as to avoid her eyes slanting directly into his. She only knew for certain that she waited for his answer to make its way to her. Finally. "I've sent it several times. Didn't get nothing back."

"Are you sure you sent it to the right address?" She was conscious of her forcefulness of inquiry and when he answered, "I'm sure," she opted to probe no further, deciding not to push him, not then in any event, but surmised with absoluteness that he lied. Tempted to catch him in a falsehood she opened her mouth as if about to say something, on the brink of asking him to repeat the address, but then calculating that he actually knew it withheld her question, figuring that in times past he likely had gone by her home repeatedly.

Their proximity would from there on become a game of cat and mouse, Anatole Wutherington combining her wit and intelligence to trick her captor into a mistake, perhaps the lowering of his guard, the effect allowing her to escape; and Osgood Nesbitt continuing his unbending dominance over his captive and holding her against her will, whose purpose she could not discern but guessed and shuddered. A girl of exceeding intelligence she stood in the upper one percent of a sizeable class in school marks; not to mention the superiority of her athleticism, the best oarsman on the rowing team, the best of the team at running the one hundred yard dash, and that she had spent a great many hours in the woods and back country with her father canoeing and hunting. Osgood Nesbitt, by and large did not equal these assets, his physique short and on the heavy side, a mite less tall than his captive and according to the records dug up after the kidnapping was over his employers tabbed him as a journeyman machinist by trade, and that he worked three years for them in their Minneapolis plant. He had worked for another firm in a small town in Illinois — but for an abbreviated duration. It could not be determined where he lived exactly, that is to say, not his exact residence by street name and street number. He was fired from his last known job. One profile read that he appeared to be a sluggish thinker, depicted traits of hardheadness and unsociability, and tended to be a loner. Whether or not he was the man once seen at night sprinting through a church yard stark naked could never be authenticated. A report related that when talking to someone he seldom altered his expression, a sort of placid and empty look, this feature complimented by a pair of cold opaque gray eyes which were implanted below two overgrown shaggy brows. A person of enormous appetite he ate voluminous quantities, tending to be substantially overweight and clearly out of condition as evinced by his excessive sweating and hard deep breathing upon movements of suddenness. .

Such a man in part held Anatole under his grip, which she now began to decide that she must contrive a way to break if she expected ever to regain her freedom.

A little more time passed. Reaching over that morning as the daylight squeezed through the cracks she pulled out the string from the second shoe so far untouched and tied another knot, then began also to count the many knots in the string belonging to the first shoe, adding to this number the one she'd just tied. "Mercy! I've been here one day over thirty. What can I do? Why don't they come get me? What is this, this, this person up to? Why doesn't he let me go? Sinking to her knees she broke into weeping, deep heavy sobs pouring forth. But they ceased as quickly as they started. "No, no, no, Anatole. You must not do this. It won't help. Keep your spirits up. You know you have to keep your spirits up." She discovered how she might by every once in awhile resurrecting little short lived feats of reverie. They came to her mostly just before she fell off to sleep, surrounded and absorbed by the imponderable darkness, thinking, thinking, not of the peculiar monster who lay not many feet away in the space next to hers — for she through sheer will had banished him from mind — but now, alarmless and unfretted, about the murmuring rain falling softly on the roof, this taking her swiftly across the gaps of time to the backwoods where at an earlier age she lay in the dryness of the tent under warm cozy blankets that her father had spread over her — "good night darling" — not dropping off to sleep, not then, too arrested by the underbelly of the wallowing canopy while the fire from the portable wood stove died away and with it the flame born shadows. The rain quit falling shortly before daylight. At midmorning they ate breakfast while sitting around an open fire, called on by the game warden, a friend of her father's, who declined to ask him for a show of his hunting license, but accepted the hospitable invitation to sit down and eat and when he left they went canoeing. Sighing, she turned over.

Increasingly Osgood Nesbitt started leaving the lair, not daily but more than normal, careful to tie her wrists before going for fear she might manage to escape. Though realizing that he did not by any stretch possess her quickness of intellect she nonetheless told herself that his cunningness and suspiciousness perhaps made up for his lacking and that his intuition ever alerted him to be watchful of her contrivances. He would stay gone for an hour or two at a time it seemed to her, returning with a preponderance of articles of use, soap, clothes for her — a good many and varied — food, and most recently collected, stolen she suspected, an assortment of attire which he left at the opening of the cubicle where she stayed and slept. Not uttering a word he merely set them on the flooring. On the outset he had not equipped the cubicle with a door. Among these articles it seemed to her there existed a pilot's uniform. After repeatedly glazing her fingers over its surface the idea dawned that the garment could be of badly needed use, for lately he started to look at her with increased intensity, with dark foreknowing eyes, devouring, as she made her way attending to pre assigned chores in the kitchen. What did it mean? "Ah! I tremble." While still suspicious he had now begun to allow her to roam around without staying glued to her side, relaxing his grip almost imperceptivity, little by little, a freedom which she relished but which she allowed herself sparingly, for too often, especially when daylight stole through she appeared plain in his sight and this she dreaded and feared. She would wear the uniform, a straggly and loose garment, more than sufficient for covering her well proportioned figure, and just before they descended the stairs that night she slipped it on. Seeing it the next morning as the daylight sifted through the windows Osgood Nesbitt appeared displeased but spoke no irritable remarks. While he prepared the breakfast she went to the ladies room, a routine which she'd begun without his approval or accompaniment. These visits she took often, but with limitation so as to not evoke his alarm. The ladies room was more than a place for attending to one's disposal imperatives; it was in fact a place of enjoyment, a pleasant respite, well decorated with portraits of nature hanging from the walls and furnished with high back s and two yellow sofas and a great mirror. It too was equipped with a shower stall. She yearned to take one. But the idea of him breaking in and catching her nude stirred her terror. "I wouldn't dare." This morning the room looked daintily pretty and smelled of the sweetest scent. A vase of red roses sat on a narrow elongated coffee table styled of Florentine renaissance. The late afternoon maintenance crew from the previous day cleaned it well and sprayed. She didn't know why it swarmed upon her, such being a sudden presence of nostalgia, bringing a gush of images of her bedroom back home. "It has to be the colors in here that does it, so soft and tender and feminine." And then she began to cry. "If I could hear my Momma's voice just once, just once. But I can't." That is all she allowed herself, then crumpled onto the soft pretty sofa nearest her and stretched her arms as far as they would reach, and her legs too. "Oh! This seems like Heaven." And laid there for another moment, but only for a moment, dreading but knowing that the serenity of her fantasy must end, and so pulling herself together daubed her tear stains and washed her face and tried to regain her composure. "Take it easy Anatole. Even the darkest night has its stars, don't you remember? Calmness, patience. Bide your time. A break will come your way." Opening the door she begrudgingly left the soothing comforts of what had become her temporary haven of retreat and steeled herself to face another day of madness.

She sat down and began to fill her plate and they began to eat, he sensing an alteration in her mood, taking little short snappy glances at her as he gobbled a mouthful. She missed not one of them upon her, knowing without seeing, but refused in her freshly nettled frame of mind to look back, done purposely as a subtle infliction of punishment. She knew now from experience that she could easily prick his psyche and that it plainly hurt him when she shut him out, and for the duration of breakfast she quit her attention of him altogether, her eyes now shifting off and on the windows which were admitting a glimmer of early daylight. Already having shed their cloak of gold she saw the browning trees, and heard the rumble of street traffic rise and fall, and the tooting of horns, and maybe a ripple of children's laughter on their way to school, though far too early for that, and all this, these endearing sights and sounds, refueled in her being a desire to break free from the cruel plight of bondage in which fate chose to cast her. She felt it powerfully, rage, and an equally powerful tendency to scream and lunge to the doorway yet brushed the idea aside at the moment of its birthing, envisioning that the attempt might or would lead to sure suicide, for he'd catch her as she strove desperately to open the door knob which he earlier locked, and that in his anger no telling what. "He'd go the limit Anatole to keep you, if not for money then in his screwy brain for companionship, even as a lover, the thought of which makes you sick to your stomach; yet consider what you are up against — and wait, wait, wait for an opening for your escape. It will come. At this game you're the better of the two. You can beat him."

She looked at him now. "Have you mailed the letter to my father? You said you would. Some days have passed you know. He'll pay you as soon as he gets it. And I'll not tell a soul about you," this last remark an unintended slip that she instantly wished she'd left unsaid, knowing that he treated it as a hollow promise which could never be lived up to. But there was more. "As I said earlier you can drop me anywhere you please, or simply turn me loose. I know how to get home."

Osgood Nesbitt heard her, giving the pretense however that her words flew over his head, gulping down an oversized bite from his second helping, practically another plate full, while simultaneously not looking up. "I'll mail the letter tonight," he at last murmured.

Flabbergasted, frustrated, and visibly angered she would have loved to fly at him with bitter scorching blasts that he lied, that he'd never mailed the first letter he promised to mail and wouldn't this one. "What is in this man's head? Doesn't he want the money? No he doesn't want the money. It's me. It's me he wants. I'm his fetish, the victim of a sexual predator. And that scares me to death." Excluding the ordinary person who would have seldom stumbled across the terms, Anatole Wutherington, a prodigious reader of literature, distinctly understood their every meaning, happening some time previously upon materials treating of fetishism dating back to long ago eras when in certain circles of Europe writings of the subject were prolific and widespread. Alexandre Guilllaume Mousier de Mossy depicted in his 1771 play, *The True Mother* (La Vraie Mere), the title character rebuking her husband for treating her as merely an object for his sexual gratification. "Are your senses so gross as to look on these breasts — the respectable treasures of nature — as merely embellishments destined to ornament the chest of women?"

"It's in his weird imagination to enslave me," said Anatole, "and has enslaved me. He's more twisted and unbalanced than I ever presumed. No, not really. I stand to be corrected. From the very start I saw into his contorted derangement."

But she refused to let the topic of the letter die irrespective of the prospect of inciting him to do her harm, employing the best of her negotiating capabilities and so — , "I'll tell you what Osgood. My father would love to see my handwriting. He dearly would, and would recognize it at once as mine. So what do you say to my drafting some words appealing to him to pay you off? And he will too. In a minute he will."

"I'll think it over." She grasped from the tone of his voice his discomfort with the question, that he wanted not to answer it but to do so was better than not, for it bothered him most discomfortingly to sit in silence and struggle with arranging what he should say when he knew she awaited a response.

"How much are you asking?"

"For what?"

"For the ransom. How much money are you asking? I haven't at any time heard you mention how much."

Again he delayed. Eventually, after rolling his eyes around in his head, "$25, 000."

"Oh he'll pay it without the least hitch. You can be assured. I'll draft a copy and give it to you for mailing," she said with elevated spirit, giving him no time for refusal.

The next night after supper he handed her a pencil and paper and asked if she still wanted to write her father a ransom letter—"Oh yes," faking excitement—, instructing her to set the sum of $25,000 as a demand for her safe return and that she would call him on a night not far removed designating a place for him to drop the money. He further asked her to tell her father definitely not to call the police and that after he picked up the money he would call them himself and then release her. None of this she believed; nevertheless, in the appearance of lifted buoyancy she took the pencil and paper and went to the ladies room to write the letter, explaining that there she could see better by the candlelight, thus making her work easier and neater. Very quickly she drafted the letter, the several minutes spent thereafter sitting or lying on one of the yellow sofas in the enjoyment of studying the paintings hanging from the walls and sniffing the fragrance of fresh flowers which the late afternoon maintenance folks plentifully set out before signing off.

He waited by the door as she came through. "Why did you take so long?" he gruffly asked.

"You wanted it done right didn't you?" When he took the letter he began to run up and down it with laboring eyes, sheepishly glancing over at her, visibly nervous, and then she discovered what she'd come to suspect in the several days past. "He can't read. My Lord, he can't read."

At this he bent over and reached for the attaché satchel which he had set next to the wall and stuck the letter into one of the compartments, saying something to the effect that he planned to mail it in the early part of the next morning while away on errands.

Mrs. Wutherington still wept continually, more pitiably, her husband's attempts to console her with urging pleas not to give up hope proving of no worth in lessening her grief and torment. He said to her with conviction in his tone that he just knew that Anatole was all right but this too went for naught. The Chief Magistrate paid call as much as his job demands afforded, once a week, as compared to everyday when the daughter first turned up missing. He could speak but few words of assuagement. In the depths of his sentiments he felt great pity for the wife, who he saw hurting indescribably, but convinced himself as well that he'd given his best to apprehend the kidnapper, if indeed there existed a kidnapper. "Was it an outright murder, a killing for revenge against the father by some crank, or disgruntled employee, who contrived in his head that the father purposely caused him wrong, with the body thrown in the lake or taken to another state and dumped into a marsh or some quarry? Or a dozen other things could have befallen the girl. Only God knows. Every prospect we've seen into has led to a dead end. Not a scratch of anything. This case is wearing me out," he uttered, raising his hands in disgust. "But I can't complain. Look at what it's doing to the father and mother." To his staff he feigned a confident air, extolling them to keep looking to uncover something of promise, reminding them in addition, as if it were one last emotional appeal, that this could be their own daughter, expressing at the finish that he perhaps ought not to have said as much because he knew these thoughts were already in their hearts.

A detective specialist of the Chief Magistrate's staff derived the idea of using trained canines to track the girl. They began by exposing some of Anatole's clothing to the animals for sniffing, following from there a course leading to various and sundry buildings —, sheds, and shacks, and old fading warehouses, living out the decadent years of their lives in sectors of the city that seemed to be of a nature conducive to someone seeking a seldom noticed unattended recluse, for whatever the purpose. A squad of policemen with dogs were dispatched on foray to search for her, and after trial upon trial, without results, wandered by chance into the construction site of the Catholic Church where Osgood Nesbitt held his captive, not in the wildest believing or sensing they were close. Anatole could hear the commotion, the whining of the dogs and the quickened chatter of their masters, as could Osgood, who crawled fast on his all fours to where she lay and there clamped the palm of his ruddy hand firmly over her mouth. "Shhhhhhh. Not a squeak. I don't want to hurt you. But I will." Understanding that Osgood now found himself in a precarious strait she did not doubt the seriousness of his threat. Clearly, the nearness of the police aroused fear in the man. Then there unfolded on the scene one of the oddest occurrences, whereon one of the dogs climbed half way up the steps leading to the catwalk, whining and yelping in a semblance of confused abjectness, until stopping dead still, then quietly slithering away. "What the hell brought that up," his master let out, taking it to be nothing of relevance, likely the scent of a rat with a gut full of poison, when the dog descended. The commotion soon grew muffled and died away. They were gone. When Osgood lifted his hand from Anatole's mouth she gasped for breath, and gasped once more, deep and labored, her throaty coughing frightening him to ask if she would be all right, and movingly showed relief when she answered yes. She wished with every fiber within her that she had yelled out, "Here I am," in that span when she could have, reasoning that she let a golden opportunity slip away, yet contending that to have attempted such a feat would have bordered on the fringe of danger in the extreme. "If I'd done it I'm afraid that would have been my end. I pray they'll come back. They were close. I'm sure they were looking for me." As time dissolved she suffered not more or less, each day and night nearly the same, and with Spartan fortitude and discipline endured the drudging routine over and over, descending the steps and across the courtyard garden to the area of the kitchen, there spending the night — much better than the daytime it occurred to her — the next morning her captor escorting her back to the attic. Each time they returned she hated him more. The idea that someone could enslave another as he was enslaving her gnawed savagely to reduce her instincts of civility. It even ran through her to attack him in the kitchen with a knife when he unsuspectingly turned away, obsessively rehearsing the stealthy maneuver in her imagination, this being to quietly lift the weapon from the drawer or grab it when it lay in sight on the kitchen table and go at him so quickly that he could not effectively counter with a defense. But each time. "No Anatole. You can't do that. It's tempting but you can't. You can't kill him with a knife even though he deserves it. It's not in you. And the odds are greatly against your succeeding if you tried. But there is an exception. If he should try to violate you, to force himself on you kill him, if you have the necessary weapon and can. Any woman would, and have the Lord's blessing. He didn't put women on earth to tolerate evil."

Some days and nights were better than others, but none of them free of suspense and fear of what Osgood Nesbitt might do if something set him off. She nervously speculated that it could be anything. More and more she set about improvising schemes that could conceivably lead to her escape, taking with her strips of concealed toilet paper smuggled from the ladies room as they retraced themselves to the attic. There, she would poke thinly torn pieces through the cracks in the wall using a fingernail file smuggled also from the ladies room. She hoped these fragments, white as they were and as many as there were, would be curiously seen strewn across the grounds. But her clever devise failed to yield reward. No one noticed, or if so perhaps took the sight of it all as a prank of youths. Her ordeal by slow gradient degrees took an increasing toll, sapping her strength and will and there were moments when she felt she might go mad; too strong however to fall prey to despondency, bouncing back with more grit than ever to face her calamity and bide her time and discover or invent a way to freedom. Eventually, after each dinner and breakfast she inherited the lot as assigned by Osgood to clear and wipe the table, which she saw in an instant as another opportunity and so acted to employ its use, raking a few morsels of food onto the kitchen floor, her fingers crossed that the morning cleaning crew might see them sooner or later and report to their superiors that something fishy was going on. This too came to no avail, apparently, but she kept at it. "Why not? It's better than trying nothing at all. Besides, he can't seriously suspect me of being up to something if he notices. He can only rebuke me for sloppiness at the most and untidiness at the least." The plot of leaving a note at a place where it might be found by the work crew or the officials of the clergy lit also upon her, which briefly would read, "I am Anatole Wutherington. I'm held hostage here. You can find me in the attic of the new construction site. Please help me. Go to the police." Yet overturned the contrivance when each time filtering it through. "Too risky," she would finally decide, of notion that he might somehow trip across the message. "What is left for me to consider," she contemplated searchingly, "I've exhausted my wits." But frustrated as she was, and angered, she returned to the drawing board of her fertile mind.

Again she turned to counting the knots in the second shoe lace, her fingers telling her now that shed had endured one month plus twenty five days of captivity, the realization sending a shudder racing through her, and asked as she asked everyday from the start "when will this madness end," but seeing no end. Words were not so far conveyed from Osgood Nesbitt that he mailed the letter to her father, nor did she have faith that he honored his promise, believing the opposite, and of the conviction that to mention the matter to him at any time further was useless, doggedly convinced at this intermission that his purpose in holding her did not have an inkling to do with money. Much within her the likelihood stirred again of the police returning and that there would emerge the awesome cold prospect of her captor going to extremes rather than give her up, even if he realized that he himself stood on the brink of extinction. And that if she were thereby endangered she should be prepared to somehow fend him off. In spite of the threat that it might pose to her, she hoped and prayed that the policemen with their sniffer dogs would revisit the church and this time be more persistent. On their last search they approached so very close. "They're looking. Every hour. I know they are. They'll break through. Just have patience." The cumulative strain had exacted an awesome toll, her patience badly depleted, the deduction naturally surfacing that only a degree of will still resided in her to live much longer in the hell that lay ahead. It was a good thing perhaps that she did not know then of that with which she would soon come face to face. On the sixty first day Osgood departed on an errand, staying for some stretch, two hours she estimated, during which it sprang to her to test the cords that bound her wrists. He chose not additionally to bind her. Straining and pulling and working her hands first one way then another she after some length and effort broke free, while exerting her utmost to listen for the stealth of his foot steps. Instantly she made for the door. "Please! If it will only open!" But the door knob stubbornly refused to turn and no tools were at her disposal with which to batter the lock apart. Even if tools were available the chances are she could not have opened the door, for on the front side a heavy slide bolt of iron was in place, Osgood having slid it into a securing position upon leaving. She tried but to no avail.. Her spirits were crushed. "Oh, terrible. I thought I had a chance." Now, anticipating that she might hear him at the door at any minute, she would hurry and work with the cords in an effort to retie them so as to give the appearance of their gripping as tightly as when he left. Osgood as of late seemed increasingly nettled, sulking and unwilling to talk, affected of scowling mood, and this profoundly bothered her. In every tedious way she strove to be cautious not to upset him more. The measure of his foul temperament loomed close at hand, for when he returned there came a hard rattling vibration as he closed the door, a sign of irritation, and that it portended disturbing news. She waited. His heavy chest exuding spurts of noisy breath he lost no time barging into where she sat. In his hand he held a flashlight, at once shining it into her face and then along her arms, bending lower as if attempting to see something more telling, her wrists and the cords that bound them. Then in contorted anger — .

"You untrusting little wench. You've tried to break free. The cords are loose."

In a fit of hysterics, his usual coarse voice ascending primitively into high piercing shrieks, he struck her face with his open hand, turning her sideways, but awed and startled by her retaliation in that same current of events. Angered rather than cowering, she lashed out, her hands now enfolded into fists and struck with stunning force, knocking him backwards, the flashlight thudding against the ceiling, ricocheting to the flooring. Primed to fight she reached frantically for her fingernail file, readying to defend herself by any tactic at her disposal.

"My only weapon. Where is it? Oh where is it?" She would jab the finely tapered point of it into his eyes, her only hope she thought as she scrambled desperately to find the precious device. But the fingernail file averted her search, in the furor a foot kicking it from where she knew it lay hidden. It was not needed as things turned out. Osgood was so thoroughly taken aback by her unexpected furiousness, together with the blow she landed against his jaw, that he for a brevity sat still and quiet, the heavy breathing coursing in and out of his chest yielding the only sound.

"Sorry I hit you. Sorry I did."

Only that. Then crawled through the opening to his own cubicle and to the doorway and got up and opened the door and passed through, locking it as he left.

She breathed a sigh. "Oooooh! So close. He could have gone into even greater rage and beaten me to a pulp and might next time. Why did he so suddenly fill up with an air of suspicion? For the life of me I can't imagine. Coincidence I guess." Lying awake for hours she sorted through her dilemma, sure with good reason that his inscrutable workings of mental process were worsening. "I've got to do something. But what?" He stayed the full day away, Anatole wondering where he might have gone — maybe just outside the door, listening, — and if when he came back he would be either settled and calm or torpid and angry.

All seemed to go well with Osgood upon his return, for the next few days his temperament suitably behaved, going out of his way to treat Anatole with much improved politeness, no longer irritable or possessed of threatening mood, but quiet and pensive, consumed by something far off and deep, which at first struck her curiously. If not strange. Then she understood, keenly associating such change of disposition with an alteration of his routine, taking notice that most recently he had started to venture out onto the catwalk at early morning, before daylight, after they made their way back from breakfast. The same as him she began to hear the voices of men and the sharp clang of equipment ascending from the courtyard garden where construction workers were hard at their tasks. She heard them on the day she freed her wrists. The practice of the crew was to arrive each day after dawn scarcely broke through. They could be plainly seen from the catwalk but the angle of the catwalk precluded them from easily seeing it, or the shadowy figure of a man looking down at them, pondering, measuring. But the figure of a man neglected to be watchful in another respect. The door to the attic was left open, and left as such each morning when he went outside, from which Anatole could see his eyes glued to the workmen, focused with riveting concentration, his awareness of the open door and his captive altogether vacating his senses.

Was it a stroke of divinity? If so it happened so imperceptibly that it slid subtly past her sphere of consciousness. When she reflected on it; when she returned to her home after the ordeal passed, the voice speaking from her soul attested that she was invisibly and unknowingly guided by her Maker to do what she did. It was the putting on of the tennis shoes that lay close by, the night before her escape. Not long in the making Osgood in the grossness of his voice called out that they were running past the hour for their meal time and that they must go down at once. But she would not budge. Not yet anyway. She would lengthen the time of departure, taking advantage of an extra few minutes to stretch and do limited exercises of her limbs, and so extended her legs to their extreme and began, not entirely aware of the direction they were pointed, but not surprised when her foot struck two rubbery objects. "Tennis shoes." And pulled them to her. "Tennis shoes. I love tennis shoes. I wear them all the time when I jog. Why have I not worn these? I know why. It's because he got them for me. I have detested them. But I'll wear them now." Realizing she'd robbed them of their laces she began instantly to take the ones from the shoes she'd worn all along as a replacement. In a jiffy she slipped them on. And then Osgood called out again that it was time. Only a faintness of daylight could yet be seen outside the attic as they started their descent,

Osgood going first, crawling across the catwalk on his hands and knees, Anatole next, waiting for him to reach the end, then it came her turn. Moving rapidly forward, abruptly stopping once then starting again, she felt the rubbery soles of her shoes grip the planking with tenacious firmness, and then smiled for the only time in two months and began to erect her design for freedom. The nerve to act stirred fiercely within her. While there had been no allowance for practice time or time for trial and error she surged with heightened excitement, but with trickles in her stomach, that all would go well.

As if nothing at all swirled in her head she sat down with her captor for the ritual meal, the candle light glowing faintly, letting her see plainly his face but keeping hers tilted at a downward trajectory into her plate lest by some aspect of her expression, a tinge of nervousness perhaps, he might read it with suspicion. She behaved normally she felt, as normally as she could coach herself to be. "He expects nothing. Oh God, let it happen as I have hoped and prayed. Don't let anything go wrong. Tomorrow morning be certain that the workers come as usual, and fix it so that Osgood is standing in the center of the catwalk holding to the side rail looking down on them. I have striven unutterably hard and gone through so much. I can't handle a lot more. I pray that you will not fail me." The night passed. She had sat for most of it pretending to read a magazine left by someone, by a clergyman she reckoned, and once went to the ladies room, not washing, not even washing her face, taking every precaution not to delay and thereby arouse him. There were times when she started into conversation, picking topics of lightness that she had learned he liked. She remembered this night well, as vividly as the sunset she said, her last one, and that before daylight they ate and left for the attic and crawled in. She would not lie down. She sat. Alert, nervous, and poised for what she prayed would come to pass. It was only minutes away. As the light crept onto the catwalk Osgood raised upward and opened the door, and went crawling out to take his position by the side rail, soon the workmen arriving, their chatter and the banging of equipment elevating to the vaulting, lilting clearly to her hearing. She had eased stealthily to the side of the attic opening, there hidden from view, the keen anticipation of escape throbbing through her veins, waiting, until at once something inside said, "now," then sprinted with deer like velocity onto the planking, in the minutest second coming upon him, his back turned toward her, fully intending to flash by to the steps beyond and downward to safety — into the arms of the workmen. But he startled, an involuntary response to the sudden rumble of two streaking rubber shoe soles. He had begun to turn around, his animal instincts supplying the warning. Too late. Barreling into him with full momentum she sent him crashing through the side rail, for which he reached in vain to save himself, screaming as he plunged to his death against the crating of jagged raw lumber at rest three stories below. Anatole heard him and yet didn't; maybe her ears but not her brain, which, as she hurdled through thin air in that tiny miniscule of a second acted, in conjunction with her primitive instincts, to find a way to save her. The blow against him had thrown her to the opposite side of the catwalk and off, the galvanized piping affixed to the girder upholding the planking the only straw left, jutting out just enough, allowing two supple hands of youthful quickness to thrust outward and clasp it as if jaws of steel, and then,"ummmph," a kind of grunt or gasp as she extended full length, there hanging suspended in imminent danger halfway across the catwalk, ten feet left between her ebbing strength and safety. "You will not die here Anatole. Not this way. Not after all you've gone through. Pull yourself together. One more trial and you can go home." With grit of uncommon strain and instance of mind she would save herself. Calling on her innermost reserves she little by little walked slowly but surely with her hands to the first stair rung, once there muscling herself up and over. "I made it, I made it," she said in an exclamation of triumph as she gasped for breath. And on regaining herself, "Hey down there," she rang out, "I'm Anatole Wutherington. I've been kidnapped. I'm Anatole Wutherington. Come get me." The workmen seeing her hand walk to safety had stared in horror and disbelief, some already before she reached the stairway starting to run to her. "It's Anatole Wutherington. Merciful Lord. Thank you." Reaching her the men behaved aghast. Some began to cry. And then every man cried, pouring out big heavy sobs that started deep. "Child. Darling. You are safe. Thank God. We've looked everywhere for you." Standing erect from where she rested Anatole attempted to descend the steps on her own, though not to be, one very ponderous man lifting her into his arms and carrying her down to the last rung and then some, holding her as if she were a baby and would not put her down even then, not until the police and ambulance arrived. That would only take minutes.

The foreman sent men over to inspect the body of Osgood Nesbitt prior to the ambulance getting there.

"Well?" — as soon as they got back.

"A broken neck, and the side of his face crushed."

"When Anatole is cared for and the police have said what they need to, tell the ambulance crew to do something with him."

She had come home now. It was over, the tears and tumult of rejoining her family over too, but not the fear of the shadows lurking underneath, the mother afraid to leave her daughter for a single minute, the father driving from his office at much repeated intervals throughout the day just to check on her, both parents neurotically anxious every minute but striving to overcome the after effect. Anatole did well, astonishingly unfazed, strong as she had been strong throughout her ordeal, the mother on her way to coping but needing time, sometimes gripped by nightmares, terror stricken in her dreams, gasping and screaming.

"Momma, Momma. Here I am. I'm all right. I'm back. I'm right here beside you. Wake up darling."

A drama of irony, daughter holding mother in her arms, consoling, the natural role of mother holding and comforting daughter reversed.

When Anatole reached home they all expected her to stay in seclusion, until overcoming the shock, the neighbors anxious to visit and pay respects, and with carefully chosen phrases offer condolences. But held back. On the very next Sunday she was seen in church, dressed in her usual robe of gold and brown singing with the choir, and afterwards, on leaving the sanctuary, chatting and embracing with folks of the congregation with an undiluted display of her customary ebullience. "She's a Gibraltar," they all said. "She shows no marks of the slightest that she's suffered."

And that is the way her life went for the longest. In time people began to adapt to the memory of the tragic event and went on with their lives just as she did hers, seeing her on occasions at the great mall in the center of the city, in their repertoire of recall hanging on to bits and pieces of the tragic episode, feeling a natural urge to bring up the subject with her, yet considerately refraining. So it faded from the consciousness of the general public as much as it could fade, but faded none in the staunch and unrelenting visage of my grandmother, who passionately talked about it with me until her final day.

Some few weeks passed, perhaps a month after Anatole's return home, and the Chief Magistrate felt it time to interview her. He had patiently delayed, as anyone and all agreed, exercising particular care not to rush, as he had advised himself, and to use the utmost of delicateness in asking if she minded joining him in his office for an exploratory session. She agreed. She was there. Sourly disliking the necessity of fulfilling this part of his job he cleared his throat, uttered a silent profanity, and proceeded with business.

"Darling we're so proud of you we could burst. All of us."

If she did not smile she came close. "Yes sir. I know. The people are wonderfully kind."

"As they should be."

She only looked into his eyes and this time smiled softly, curiously anticipating what next she would hear.

"If you don't mind dear, let me ask a few questions. My job you know. I have to debrief you as I would anyone."

"I know. Please do."

"Well first. The two shoe strings. Tell me how they have a bearing, how they fit in your story?"

"The shoe strings. Oh! My friends. My lifeline; through them I kept my sanity. I simply tied knots in them and counted the knots as time passed, which let me know the days I had been locked up. To know this was to help me keep going."

"Fighting?"

"Yes."

"Ha. Who else could have thought to do that but you? So ingenuous."

"Was there something else sir?"

"Well, I think there is. If you will allow it. It, it, —."

"I will."

"Thank you. Then I'll go on. It concerns something that may be touchy. Whether or not he violated you. It's important for the record if you don't mind."

"For the record if I don't mind. And if I do mind do I have a choice?"

"If you mind then the question was not asked."

"But it was asked and I don't mind. No, not once did he bother me in that way. I continually feared he might. I was afraid to death of him. And I think sir if I could have — if he had attacked me — I would have tried to kill him."

"As you should have. But tell me this. What reason did he have for taking you hostage? Do you know? I thought for awhile, in fact to the very last, that it could have only been for money. But no ransom note ever cropped up. None. I expected one, hoped for one as bad as the news might be. Do you know of any message that he sent to us or to your father?"

"It wasn't sent. He told me that he would send out notes to my father but I knew he lied. Once I urged him to let me write a letter to my father pleading for the money to be sent, $25,000, the amount he said he demanded. It was never mailed. I know that for sure."

"But still I'm confounded. Why did he kidnap you? It looks to me like, if I may answer my own question, that it centered on something like companionship. Was that it? Perhaps."

"About it. Something like that. Obviously he had affections for me. He seemed to be driven by two minds, one with a good kind side and the other by derangement, not exactly by evil but by derangement."

"I see. That's how you saw him, experienced him I should say. You would know more than anyone else. Two sides. Hmmmm. A schizophrenic, our learned colleagues over at the university would tell us. A dangerous man. You could have lost your life darling. And you knew you might unless you played the game of cat and mouse just right and you did. You won. You're the smartest girl I have ever known."

After they had talked on for awhile, the Chief Magistrate seeking to learn of other things that she could reveal gestured as if bringing the interview to an end but declined, hanging on for at least a trifle longer. He wished to pursue another aspect of the subject, only briefly, he assured, which fell not in the legal bounds of why they were there, but it seemed so personally compelling to him that he found himself unable to resist opening it up.

"Anatole, before you go will you allow me one last thing."

"Of course. What is it?"

"Quite a story has been told here, a rare one. I trust that I'm not out of place in revealing that if ever it should be written I would like to be permitted to recommend the title."

"The title! And what might that be?"

"Tale of the Two Shoe Strings."

A shadow of a smile spread softly, then lessened into pensiveness, then returned with a glow. "I like it."

With some measure of regret I learned once that the Chief Magistrate's goal eluded him, his pleasure blocked by my own exertions; but he could not have cared, for he had long gone on to his Maker.

When I had attained to the age of twenty five and she had reached thirty I went back to that city and attended Sunday service at the massive Lutheran Church with its decorous walnut newels spiraling to the balcony level of which Anatole was a member dating back to before she attained to age five. The urge had writhed within me for the longest to do this and finally I did. I found what I came to find. There she stood off to the left singing in the choir dressed in her robe of gold and brown — I knew that had to be her — a singularly beautiful woman as my grandmother would have agreed. I asked someone sitting next to me to identify her by name and according to the position she occupied among the others.

"Yes, that's Anatole Wutherington. Do you know her?"

"Kind of. I met up with her in earlier years."

Unknown to my senses I had begun to gather bits and pieces even then to write of her story. Now I have. She was a very brave girl.

Road to a Record Deal

HE STRUMMED his first chord to impress his cousin Eugene and sang the title to a song. "Whaaaang," and "*Jole Blon*," and then did it again.

"Is that all?" asked Eugene, expecting more though ignorant of guitars and singing.

"Well, yeah. What I strummed is a chord and what I sang is a song that I learned from our first cousin who not long ago got back from the army as you know and sang and played at the family reunion."

The original Cajun version of *Jole Blon* is a brief allusion to a pretty blonde who has left the singer and moved back in with her family, now, or soon thereafter in the arms of another man. The singer, to save face possibly, or actually believing in himself, boasts that there are plenty of women, pretty blonde women too, that he can have any time he wants. Artists sometimes combine English and French verses in the song, walking a fine line between Cajun and Western swing rhythms, which evoke a strain of music enjoyed by mid century oil field workers — a lilting unadulterated dance hall music with an emphasis on Saturday night waltzes, stomps, and two steps.

"But is *Jole Blon* all there is to sing? Don't it have other words?"

"It does. But *Jole Blon* is all he taught me so far; it's the title. Said he'll teach me the whole of it when he can work out the time, down to the last line."

"Is that thing yours?"

"No, it's not mine. He just left it with me for awhile to mess around with, owing to his having more than he needs laying scattered about in his house, cause he collects guitars through swaps and buyings and always ends up with a big advantage, sometimes gaining two for one."

"What's a chord?"

"It's a sound. It's what I just strummed. It happens when you grip the strings to a guitar in a certain way with your fingers and with certain other of your fingers you swipe across them."

"Ah."

"There's a passel of chords to a guitar, I don't know how many, but many, and I'm going to learn them all, and then I'm going to be famous, everywhere, everybody hearing me play and sing. But singing be reminded is what I want to do deep down most. Picking a guitar and playing chords, when I learn them, is going to be way back there in the dust. Singing is it. I want to be famous someday as a singer. Real bad."

J. T. Conrad had reached his eleventh year of life; so had his cousin Eugene, only two months behind him who looked up to J. T. with puppyish admiration? That was five years in the past and now he had turned sixteen.

An amateur talent contest, a variety show, was to be held at Clovis, not by any yardstick on par with the variety shows staged by the radio stations of national scale, but yet a variety show and J. T. had set his mind hard on competing. But only to sing. They took him on to compete on the strength of a recommendation of an acquaintance. Another competitor, only a scant older than himself but old enough to own a driver's license, planned to go and volunteered to pick him up at Whiteface where he lived with his parents, a distance of eighty miles from Clovis where Station KICA would broadcast the event and furnish the judges, the radio officials careful to mention in the advanced publicity that contestant winners were to receive no rewards, prizes or money, for their participation — only an announcement and a piece in the newspaper of the winner.

"Reward! Who needs or wants a reward?"

These were the unselfish cavalier sentiments of J. T. as the upcoming event began to swirl wildly in his impression, the only thing of essence being to compete, as for as he was concerned, although there emerged a release of news information two days before, which baffled everybody, that prizes were to be awarded to each of the winners after all, a chocolate cake and a sum of three dollars.

When notified through the mail, by post card, that the officials had chosen him as a participant he erupted into a state of unrequited rapture that ran for the portion of the day remaining and into the night, a vision swelling in his head of a singing cowboy on his way to radio and recording stardom, and that movies in due course would catch up. He could see these magnificent achievements as plain as day, his first step to fame, even going so far that night in the wee hours, just before succumbing to sleep, that he must take his guitar along, for he assumed or was told by someone supposedly savvy in the music industry that a singer at like contest should accompany himself with a musical instrument or be supported by a small band or at least by a tunesmith who could pick. Without anyone in his family aware of his intents J. T. began his preparations, what he would wear on his person, and the narrowing of his songs down to the one which he'd sing at the contest, among them the widespread popular tune *You Are My Sunshine,* a wholesome rendition sung by a genre of singers of the Hollywood movie culture or by family members, parents and progeny, across the Texas plains and in the hills and hollers of Kentucky and Tennessee, everywhere; and then chose another sung just as often, *South of the Border,* a lovely creation with something of a Latin rhythm, regrettably having an ending that carried a saddened refrain. The cowboy, usually a cowboy actor who sang it in the movies, passionately adored a young Spanish senorita but after leaving for north of the border stayed away excessively long, finding upon his return that she had pledged her life to the nunnery. I yi yi yi, I yi yi yi, the song ended with almost a remorseful melancholy. At the moment of first hearing it J. T. fell in love with the song, and began to love all Latin compositions, holding a lifelong inestimable respect and admiration for the composers that gave birth to this form of music. In the finale however he selected neither of the two for the contest.

Sometime earlier he managed to own a guitar, paying for it by working at odd jobs here and there, hiring out in the main to commercial turkey farmers of the area whose business had to do with slaughtering turkeys on a massive scale, his task in particular calling for dunking the carcass of the pre eviscerated fowl into a cauldron of scalding steaming water then hanging it on an ever moving wire line where with both hands he snatched and grabbed the left over feathers from the skin surface at a speed commensurate with the rate pre set by the assembly line foreman. Not a fascinating nor an inspiring occupation but a dream drove him and he wasn't to be deterred. When he purchased the guitar, a Kay brand, the price tag read $6.25, a hefty amount he thought, flinching; but he paid it, and took the next tempting step, the purchase of an instructional self teaching guide, costing a net price of 25 cents, a Mel Bley Instructional Guide to Learning Guitar, the seductive wording encouragingly appearing in bold print at the top of the cover page. It had to be a bargain he figured;

everything was a bargain back then, a loaf of bread by comparison costing but five to eight cents at the corner grocery. You could see it in his face: childish euphoria and innocence as he looked down and picked up his new possession, cradling it in his arms, turning it over and over with the tenderness of touching a baby as if inspecting for flaws, or if not that then in admiration, dragging his fingers caressingly along the smooth ivory surface, around and down, tracing the curving rich man's swimming pool shape of the frame.

"The purtiest thing I ever saw. Ain't it something Eugene?"

In his eyes there shone an attitude of awe that bore no signs of diminishment as he left the store, or for days and months to come.

Studying relentlessly he within weeks started to play a variation of chords with suitable proficiency, because he already knew a few, and concluded, as well as his friends, that he could adequately accompany himself, even better than adequately he felt, if an opportunity cropped up which required a demonstration of his skill.

"Practice, practice, practice. I've go to be good."

Not knowing the end effect his father advanced him a quarter one day for going to a movie, Gene Autry's *Public Cowboy Number One,* showing at a local theater, an experience which doggedly persevered in his heart and set off a litany of fantasies that resulted into still greater determination and began to evolve visions of emulating the much acclaimed actor of cowboy movies.

Then the post card came and now the contest. Entering the radio station control room he nervously glanced the image of the silvery shiny microphone in the center of the room with no one yet around — knowing his time would shortly arrive but fearing it — nervously contemplating whether his voice would be transmitted to the Clovis and Lubbock and even to the Whiteface listeners. And then began to pour over a raft of worries natural to a young man facing a test so crucial: "What will I sound like, suppose my voice cracks, and suppose I hit the wrong guitar string, and how close to the microphone should I stand, and how far away and how I hate the idea of that bunch of people looking in on me from the other side of that glass. But whoa! Get hold of yourself J.T. You need to concentrate on only one thing and you know what that is."

Some thirty or more contestants stood poised and ready to go, singers, yodelers, impersonators, comedians, an exhaustive array of talent he thought, the sheer numbers threatening to take up the entire morning and a huge bite of the afternoon, the singers though scheduled to appear first — fifteen in all, with three minutes a piece allowed for showing what they could do.

"Fifteen! Boy. That's a pretty good many and not everyone will win; in fact only one can and it may not be me. In fact I'm doubting it will be."

Selecting a Gene Autry song, gambling that such a choice might work in his favor, J. T. approached the microphone, more confidently than he assumed he would earlier, and with every muscle and fiber in his body straining to peak capacity launched into *I'll Never Let You Go Little Darling,* the title prompting one of the female attendants of mid life age watching from the gallery to jestfully remark afterwards, "What a serious idea from such a young growing boy," and went around herself singing some of the lines that J. T. had sung, "I'll never let you go little darling, I'm sorry that I made you cry, I'll never let you go little darling, So please don't try to say goodbye."

It worked. After standing around in the hallway for an hour after the competition ended — eyeing one another suspiciously, trying their best to force at least a half smile, "I wonder if he's the one who won it," all pretending in their facial countenances they really didn't care, but lying to themselves — the contestants finally got the news.

"You won, you won J. T.," the disc jockey standing before the entire group exuberantly announced, seemingly disregarding the others, J. T. hearing but unsure as to whether he heard correctly, reacting with virtually uncontrolled animation when the disc jockey's revelation finally sank in, jumping up and down as if he were close to sprouting wings, aimlessly darting about to first one then another, hugging and carrying on, and almost just as ecstatic when the station manager offered to let him sing on KICA each Saturday for a quarter of an hour but with no pay. He couldn't quite gather it all in.

"Lands alive! My own radio show and I'm only sixteen years old."

Marvin Greer, — a chum of J. T.'s, which his father sternly discouraged because Marvin at age twenty seemed too old for J. T. to hang around and because Marvin played and sang with a western swing band that hired out to the road houses of northern New Mexico and West Texas, — eyed the winner with a glint of jealousy. He himself entered the contest too, and lost, but nonetheless spirited over to zestfully slap J. T. on his back.

"You did it J. T. You're on your way just like you always said you'd be."

J. T. indeed won, enraptured at the congratulations stemming from the contestants as well as from the audience spectators who came forth with the usual accolades, neutral folks, who couldn't have cared an iota who won or lost — but there were a sprinkling that did, those being certain contestants who vibrantly lauded the winner upon the announcement though who now started to fade into a mould of surliness. "Bastard kid. A set up. The judges got paid off." What seemed to J. T. a celebratory event, internalizing that everyone embraced nothing but goodness and happiness for him, was but an illusion, which is so often born from youthful naiveté.

His hard earned achievement of which he was more than chesty proud excited not celebration but ill will and envy.

Marvin had said that he was on his way, high sounding encouragements that tended to instill in J. T. a more determined effort than ever to pursue his dream, though for a moment however, only for a moment, there arose in his consciousness an undertone of sobriety that forced a touch of hesitation, which he shared with friends in the latter years of his life. "The thought of the roadhouse life of the artist almost turned me around, coupled with the negative view passed to me by my father of the life of a singer, the temptations and miseries he'd have to put up with everywhere he went. The image of the roadhouse life bothered me a lot, a great deal, the major portion formed from my listening to the tales told to me by Marvin. I had actually never seen the inside of a roadhouse, so I learned what I knew of such establishments from him. Places of bad character. That's how I saw them, drunks fighting over women, and a beehive of vice — drugs and gambling and prostitution and adultery. I didn't see anything but visions of perfidious human behavior but made up my mind that I could adapt to such things, not letting them pull me down, seeing to it that my view, my dream to be a singer and the personal joy it would bring overrode. So I stuck it out; I refused to turn back."

Clovis lay better than two hours north of Whiteface, a stretch which posed a trifle of difficulty for J. T., hitchhiking a ride the only mode of getting to where he wanted to be, especially on time, and at certain hours the traffic was thinly sparse on the highway that he would have to travel. But when the motorist moved they generously displayed kindness, the sight of a tall gangly mid teen boy with coarse dark hair, dressed in blue jeans, toting a guitar, with a pleading beg on his face for a lift likely touching their sentiments.

"Where you goin boy?"

"Clovis."

"Clovis. I can haul you part of the way. As far as Morton. It's only a little ways. But that'll help won't it?"

"Oh yes. Yes sir," he returned gratefully. "I really will appreciate it."

Out of the side of his eyes, a trick that his basketball coach called split vision, J. T. stole glances of the man, deciding he'd met up with some sort of business executive dressed in a ten gallon (galon in Spanish) white hat and a white shirt and stripped pants — a very clean looking man it dawned on him, driving a late model spotless pick up, too clean to be an oil field truck. "Naw, he's no oil man. Truck 'ud be caked an inch thick with ugly brown mud if he was." He wondered what opinion the man might have of him, but in no time threw that aside, taking the view that whatever he thought couldn't be of much consequence in that he said very little to him in the miles they'd put behind.

"Screech." It caught J. T. off guard, his nose almost bumping the windshield and would have except for bracing against the dash with his hands.

"Hurtchi?" The man stopped suddenly in the middle of Morton, after missing his turn, having let his mind drift off from where it should have been.

"No sir."

"You sure?"

"I'm sure. Thanks very much for the ride," he said, as he opened the cab door and slid out, aiming for the city limits on the north side, soon to reach the edge of town where he'd stand, as he'd done before, while waiting to thumb a ride. Nearby, a half block away, there stood a diner, a night spot that daytime locals referred to as a diner, with a string of exotic neons affixed to the façade, just above the trade name House of Blue Lights, aglow and flashing on and off in spite of the mid morning hour.

Of this place he'd already taken notice during his previous brief comings and goings, never venturing close, never seeing the inside, but aware that by and large people viewed it as an establishment of questionable repute, the evidence supplied by the tempting posters in the windows depicting the beautiful streamlined figures of females clad in dresses with obvious haughty bustles and a sensual cowboy with jet black wavy hair and a waspy waist in the fashion of a flamingo dancer waiting in the wing to dance with the beautiful lady of his choice. He knew he shouldn't but that made no difference. His curiosity reigned all powerful. Edging closer, not only did he gain a sharper image of what he had seen from the more distant vantage but now could glance other smaller but colorful posters — on which some of the well known circuit pickers and singers of the region were illumed. Moving to the doorway, peeping, pausing, but holding back, then pausing again he finally poked his head inside, a whole day to pass before the gathering of the night crowds and so too the lively whirl of genuine honky tonking. Seeing no danger nor sensing any he pushed through the swinging doors and took a chair near a far corner which afforded an unimpeded view of a cluster of thirsty cowboys at the bar, well behaved at this hour, merely bursting every once in a while into a cacophony of laughter because apparently one of them said something funny. Someone fed the jukebox, a melody instantly wafting to him that he at first missed recognizing and then turned to listen with greater concentration, figuring that he might be familiar with the tune after all, but then.

"Boy, whacha doin in this joint?"

"Wha, wha — ." Startled, gazing upward into the reddish keen eyes of the local sheriff, who spotted him across the street as a hawk might a rabbit as he entered the front door, he gasped, then the huge towering man lifted him by his collar from where he sat. There was no drink to spill. Even though seeing him enter no one working the bar dared venture over to offer service, not even to ask if he'd like to have a coca cola.

"Where you from?"

"Whi, Whiii, Whiteface," he finally sputtered, his stomach suddenly feeling like frozen fire.

"Listen boy. You see that street out there?"

"Ye, yes sir."

"You git on it. You got fifteen minutes to git out of town. Suggest you head south. This ain't no place for a lad of your age. Savvy?"

"Yes sir."

Flying out the door he turned south as the sheriff advised, bound for Whiteface, moving as fast as his legs could move without asking them to run, not pausing, not even thinking to turn around and thumb a ride. "It might be the sheriff." Twelve long miles or more stretched between him and Whiteface and he would have covered the full distance on foot, like as not, except after he'd walked some substantial length a motorist pulled up offering a lift, gratefully accepted. He crawled in. More like lurched. And they began to talk. J. T. hoped he in no way reflected that he still shook from the sheriff's scare and soon figured he appeared of normal calm because the driver seldom looked his way, keeping his eyes peeled fast to the road and dwelled on things ordinary in conversation, asking where he lived and casually threw in once that it was a pretty day for hitchhiking in that no clouds were anywhere to be seen. And then it hit him: "Good Lord. I'm missing my show. It starts at one o'clock and I won't be there." After the panic lessened he pictured that the disc jockey would spin records in the wake of his absence, and then began to conjure up the lie he would tell in an attempt to explain and justify why he hadn't showed up. When the driver pulled over in Whiteface he drew a sigh of relief. But the sheriff had done him a favor and a favor for his father whom the sheriff knew, and knew J. T. also, or about him, which J. T. wasn't long in finding out. It came to him that his father earlier approached the sheriff to see after his son's welfare as he passed through Morton and in his own crude manner the sheriff did as asked, instilling enough fear into the young boy's senses to guarantee the passage of at least a few years before he paid call again on the House of Blue Lights.

Yet he would with beneficial gain return to Morton, how soon he never exactly said, but it seems to have been a year or more after the incident involving the sheriff when the famous Bob Wills and his Texas Playboys docketed at the Morton Roller Rink for a string of nightly performances. With nothing to do during the daytime the players often migrated to their favorite watering hole, an open air restaurant down street from their hotel, to have a beer, enjoy a meal, and kill time and play around with their banjos, fiddles, and guitars. J. T. had attended the show the night before. It did not occur by accident that he ventured into the restaurant the day after; doing so to seek one of them out, a particular one, Eldon Shamblin, well known for his guitar finesse, the best that ever was people swore. He sat tuning his guitar or so thought J. T. but J. T. hadn't the courage to directly approach the heralded musician, at first staying at a distance, merely observing, studying the man but after a bit summoning enough grit to kitten over to where he sat, though not unnoticed.

"Hi young man. Whatcha got there?"

"Uh. uh," the grating non syllables pushed with resistance from his throat, uncomfortably dry owing to the gravity of the excitement. "My guitar," he said — almost sheepishly.

"Ha, ha, ha, ha." But the laugh gave every appearance of kindness, in no way subtracting from his dignity. "I see you have. Here, let me look at it."

Then he took it, lifting it from J. T's outstretched arms, fondly rolling it over in search of something, J. T. thinking it to be the trademark, floored by the honor; and more honored when Shamblin began to slide his supple fingers over and up and down the strings, from which wafted a Spanish refrain, beautiful, that he recognized upon the first note as would many a Texan should they have stood beside him, for in every West Texas household there resided at least someone who could sing it. Shamblin looked up. "*Usted Pertenece A Mi Corazon.*"

"*You Belong To My Heart.*"

"Yep. That's it. Would you like to sing a line or two?"

"I guess not. I don't know the lines well enough." He lied. And later reproached himself unforgivably for letting his timidity stand in the way of doing something he would have given a hundred dollars to have done while the great man sat listening.

"Nice little guitar. Yeah, it's all right. You play much?"

"Not much. I try. I, I've been wondering if you'd teach me a chord or two."

"Why shore. Why not? Glad to young buddy."

And then Shamblin sat for an hour patiently going through the basics and adding a trite of hot licks just to show how it could be done and from there on when J. T. caught him playing at a nearby venue he generously gave of his time and skill and knowledge when asked. "I guess Eldon couldn't have ever guessed what he meant to me, and to no telling how many future generations," and would have gone on but — . "What, what Erskine?" Erskine, a long time friend, and closest, sat with him often on his front porch reminiscing, both older now, sixty five, maybe seventy, older likely; Erskine was a scholar, well read in the realm of literature, once a high school teacher, leaving teaching to set up his own accounting business. He said that teaching, staying up late struggling with lesson preparations exhausted him to the extent that no energy or freshness was left over for reading for pleasure. J. T. began to admire his intellectual capability when first meeting him and undertook over the years to read an impressive many of the books he suggested, becoming himself rather erudite in expression and word mastery.

"I was just about to ask if you knew who gave him his start just like he gave you yours."

"I don't know that. Don't think I ever asked him. And he didn't volunteer."

And then got back to where he left off. "As sure as the sun sets I can proudly attest I've forever taken pains with young people seeking to learn something to boost their craftsmanship. I hope I've paid Eldon back. He taught me loads about the guitar, but in addition something else of great importance, the essentials of kindness, a virtue that goes far beyond monetary worth, which costs absolutely nothing to give."

He kept singing for the radio station, his voice reaching as far as Lubbock and into the heartland of West Texas and northern New Mexico, spreading his name as a budding artist and consequently places of Friday and Saturday night attraction in time reached out for his talents and invited him onto their unpretentious small stages. These were the roadhouses of which Marvin told him, to which the weekend fun seekers migrated in droves — drinking, chain smoking, talking loud, perpetually erupting into raw hard laughter, and he found it not uncommon to see a woman in a polka dot dress clinging to a half drunk cowboy, a vision of comedy and pathetic raunchiness, as they groped to keep time with the slow dance tune played by the band. The roadhouses of that era were cheaply constructed edifices with alternating lights of varied colors mounted high up on the façade, seen easily at or near sundown flickering off and on for miles away, a seductive guise, a powerful magnet that cowboys and cowgirls of the surrounding region could not resist. It was likened to the nightly insect which is phototrophically drawn to a glowing lamp, unable to help itself, J. T. once said to Erskine, and that even though he saw the raucous life of the roadhouse as not a good thing he admitted that it was nonetheless something to which he lent himself as a willing accomplice.

His fame grew. So too his ambition. More and more people learned of him. .

"You're J. T. Conrad. Yeah. I've heard of you," the coarse raspy voice of Ace Ball resounded, a country music band leader and singer whose venues extended to a network of West Texas and New Mexico small to medium size towns, San Angelo, Clovis, Odessa, Lubbock, Santa Rosa, Elida, and J. T. reeled with vanity that a well known band leader of the region, far better known than himself, paid him tribute, a tribute however behind which lay a motive, which J. T. couldn't see, couldn't even guess, yet it was there, and on its way to coming out.

"Where'd you hear bout' me?" J. T. curiously asked, already sure that it had to be the Clovis radio station.

"On the radio. You sing good."

"Well, thanks," he said shyly, but unable to camouflage his elatedness over the accolade.

"Besides the radio where you singin these days? Who are you with?"

"Nobody right now." He didn't think it necessary to make it known that he'd never been with anybody and went on. "To tell you the truth, well, I was wondering if you'd have any need for a back up singer. Maybe somebody to front?"

Ace earlier signed a contract to perform for the Saturday Afternoon Jamboree in Lubbock that promoters heralded as a top flight show, and its performers, as well as the crowds, particularly liked the Sled Allen Arena, the site where the show took place. While the arena's chief purpose was to accommodate wrestling match events it all the same was a popular entertainment venue.

"I might take ya on." He rubbed his bearded face, and his eyes, eyes at once hard and friendly , but the twinkle he saw in them signaled the outcome. "Yeah. I'll let you sing with us. But no pay J. T. You do it to learn." The door opened; and right then he knew that the dream was beginning to unfold; he'd be singing for the first time with an organized well publicized sought after live band.

"Where you live J. T.?"

"Whiteface."

"Can you get here all right?"

"Ah yeah. I hitchhike all the time from Whiteface to Clovis. You know. From Whiteface to Clovis to sing for KICA."

"Okay. Show up Saturday."

The Jamboree shows ran for three hours on Saturday afternoons, but Ace invited J. T. to tag along to the lesser venues on Saturday nights and to those out on the plains where he did shows during the week, definitely on Friday nights, promising that they'd make it back to drop him off at Clovis in time to do his radio gig. Aside from the loss of sleep, things went well enough; J. T. happy, more than happy, thrilled, but still he fretted underneath that Ace hadn't asked him to sing solo, only back up harmonies. But he sloughed his disappointment aside, considering that just to be on stage singing to a crowd that truly seemed to listen amounted to an honor. He wasn't sure if they listened to the harmonies a whole lot or only a little, but either way suited him. "As Ace said, I'm learning and I have to wait for the right doors to open, the ones that lead me to where I want to be." They seemed to have done exactly that one day when out of the blue Ace announced that the Pioneer Tavern in Elida, New Mexico was taking them on for a fairly good length of stay, telling J. T. that he'd put him on the payroll if he would go.

"I'll go. I'll ask the station boss for a temporary leave." It was granted. In late afternoon while chatting once with Erskine on his front porch he said that Ace could talk anyone into believing and accepting anything. "He could add two plus two and make you believe the total summed to five. I can't deny that in my head there were some qualms against going, but I went."

By now Ace judged that J. T. had improved his guitar picking to a level that merited his filling the empty slot as the lead guitarist, this action taking place everybody figured because Ace laid out rules to which the former lead guitarist objected and fired him: and further sweetened the pot for J. T. by letting him sing solos here and there, yet kept him singing harmonies for making his own voice sound better by overlaying it with one of superior quality. But Ace was the star and stressed it with no uncertainty to his band, J. T. careful not to stir his ire by giving the appearance of upstaging, a young artist's death warrant.

Elida! What could he say? The sun beat down, the winds blew, the plains lay dusty and baking in desolation, the hotel with its fading roller shades suffered for the lack of modernity, and all this twisted into one effect meant that the only life of pleasure for the members of the band must evolve from their own picking and singing. Elida had to be grossly unappealing to a young man whose aspirations were pointed toward a recording career, toward the big city bright lights, this tiny forgotten place in no little way helpful in the realization of that dream; but yet Ace insisted that his discontent should be viewed as an essential part of paying his dues. "Everybody does son. You have to pay your dues. Nobody starts at the top. If you wanna make it to the big time you'll sing in the dives and ignore the discomfort that naturally walks along with it."

Ace tried to do especially well by J. T., sensing that something troubled him, striving among other things to boost his morale, also trying to help everyone, the young ones most singularly, but acting particularly as a father figure to J. T., nudging him aside in private to give advice when they first set foot in Elida.

"See here J. T. You need to know this right off the bat. Watch out when mixing with the crowd. Serious thangs can happen to a good looking young man. I know."

J. T. did not doubt him and from there on stayed faithfully glued to the stage, or in an otherwise perimeter designated for the band, unless notified to the contrary, sensing that the plentiful feisty Chiquita's flirtatiously taunting the rowdy cowboys gathered at the bar spelled danger, that at the least provocation a red eyed drunk could yank out a Bowie knife from inside his boots; and determined to follow Ace's counsel drew an immovable line between himself and the crowd. "You're not here to socialize boy, only to entertain," Ace had said and it stuck.

The contract period ran its course at Elida so business shifted to Santa Rosa where they were to play at Medley's Lounge, a casino of some resemblance equipped with slot machines in the larger space, and gambling tables in the backrooms out of obvious sight of the law. The stage looked fabulous, huge and clean and glitzy, the sound system pure and clear, exceeding the one at Sled Allen Arena by a no comparison margin. The crowds were unduly noisy, management seeming not to mind however and neither the band, for there seldom arose an occasion of disorder among them; business folks by and large, more controlled and politer than the social order at the lesser and smaller establishments. While they laughed loud and talked loud they drank minimally by comparison and spent lavishly as management well noticed, encouraging the band to use themselves as a marketing tool, performing at their best on stage and going among the people at intermission to mix and introduce themselves and sign autographs, if on nothing more than a piece of torn apart envelope, a complete reverse from the restrictions on which Ace adamantly insisted at Elida. For whatever the reason there were no Chiquita's.

J. T. reveled in the transition to a new atmosphere. It refreshed him. Santa Rosa lies between Tucumcari and Albuquerque, situated on the Pecos River, and brims with natural clear lakes, an anomaly in the surrounding desert terrain. After lunch he and the younger set itched to tear out for a swim in what was then known as the Blue Hole. Medley's Lounge in the usual sense could have been classified as a roadhouse but given its size and quite lavish interior, the locals proudly referenced it as a casino, and it drew the crowds to its doors in burgeoning numbers.

He wasn't sure how it happened or why it happened. He wished it hadn't. Glancing over from his breakfast one morning he detected the image of Marvin Greer on the other side of the room coming toward him.

"J. T. buddy, how are you," said Marvin, as ebullient as ever, too ebullient to have suited Mr. Conrad, J. T.'s father, who warned contemptuously that Marvin's brushes with trouble meant that he might fall into more trouble, next time more seriously, and thereby drag his son over the precipice with him. J. T. thought of his father's concerns as he stuck out his hand.

"Good. I'm good. Ouch! What a grip. Look what that slamming them spikes on that railroad job did for you last year."

"Ha, ha. You're stretching it. Good to see you."

"I echo that. But I'm jolted. You're a long way from your house. What brings you?"

"I passed through here yesterday morning on my way to Albuquerque to join a band there. Filling in for somebody. We played a gig there till eleven, then I lit out to back here. I didn't get in till late. Ace agreed to meet with me by phone and stayed up."

"I can't believe it. Must have wanted to see you pretty bad. When he's sleep raddled he's generally in a sour mood. How did he behave?"

"Okay."

"What did the meeting regard?"

"Nothing much. Actually, whether he'd use me as a fill in for awhile for Lacy your base guitar player. Lacy's wife is sick. He's asked off for a month. Ace said he'll use me in his place."

"I didn't know about this. But it's none of my business, so I wish you well Marvin. Welcome aboard."

The entire band — eight members now that Marvin joined them, and in that Lacy decided to defer leaving for another three days — slept in a chicken coop cubicle, cramped for even four, furnished by the owners of the lounge, an experience severely trying for J. T. to bear, worsening when someone began to snore to such an extreme that he got up and carried his pillow with him and slept in the lobby for that night and the next two. That was the only bad part of their stay at Medley's Lounge he said. But the torment lessened a bit when Lacy left and not long afterwards Marvin followed, who departed not because of the conditions of sleeping but because Ace grew distressingly unhappy with his performance.

"That guy couldn't even pick beans, much less a base guitar."

In the briefest while thereafter Ace handed Marvin his walking papers, telling him straightly with no hem hawing about it that he couldn't remain with the band.

"You firing me Ace?"

"You got that right. Yeah, you're fired. I gotta do what's best for the band. I'll pay ya up."

Despite his misgivings about his character J. T. nonetheless felt a touch of compassion for Marvin, sorry to see him go, yet in time would go himself, the whole band would, for Ace unexpectedly failed to come up with the venues willing to pay the price he asked, and so momentarily dissolved the band, leaving J. T. to form his own band and go back to singing on KICA. But Ace was likened to that proverbial cat, always landing on his feet, and it wasn't too terribly surprising when he showed up one morning at KICA announcing the reassembly of the band, excluding one or two old members and adding one or two new ones.

"J. T. my boy. I knew I'd find you here. Now take this seriously. I'm starting up the band again. Don't say no. I need you. It'll be like old times. Better than old times. I need you as the featured singer. My old voice is wearing out. I got wind of that before I dissolved the band, a good while before. People started to mail a snide kind of letter every once in awhile saying it sounded as rough as a bunch of gravel rocks on a hill side. And I no longer argue with that. Now it's your turn. It'll be your show. I'll just play base on the wing and stay out of the way."

"Do you mean that? You mean you want me truly to sing lead? Truly?"

"I mean it J. T. Let's hit the road."

And they did, expanding their out reach to Western New Mexico and Oklahoma, and down into Louisiana, and into Central and South Texas, staying with the pace for what amounted to two years or was it three J. T. once asked when looking back. "We were moving at full speed and it almost seemed like we'd never slow down. We didn't slow down, swoosh, all at once we just suddenly stopped. Ace was worn out; we all were. That's the way it is with the road, unhealthy eating and sleep deprivation getting to you sooner or later. I didn't mind our quitting, really. Already I teetered on the brink of doing something else and actually had started looking around. But what was I to look for? I couldn't claim any skills except singing and picking the guitar. I was stuck. But as fate would have it, after we'd hung it up as a band for going on to a month, an old idea sprang back into life. A resurrection I guess you'd call it."

Suddenly he entertained the idea again of landing a role in the movies, now more than ever, and so he approached Marvin with the notion of taking a trip to Hollywood to check things out, venturing that both could ride a horse as well as anyone out there, and sing and play a guitar, and if they hit it lucky they'd only have to sit back and watch the money roll in. Of the two it likely appeared that Marvin possessed qualities better suited for attracting the eyes of the Hollywood people as a perfect roughneck cowboy, given his football lineman frame and spike heeled boots and skin tight jeans that he forever wore. That wasn't so of J. T. Too clean perhaps, he said of himself, but still he believed an opportunity waited in tinsel town for him, and for Marvin.

"You might be right J. T."

"Sure I'm right." This time J. T. turned out to be the aggressor, not Marvin, whose characteristics of daredevil flings and debatable judgment should have compelled J. T. to draw back and look doubtingly into the implications of the scheme swirling in his head. "Problem is Marvin, I don't see how we can go unless we come up with some bucks. I'm broke."

"Yeah. Well, I'm working over at the bank and the amount of my pay is not much bigger than the size of a pea. Wouldn't help much, would it?"

The bank to which he alluded was the Clovis National Bank, a powerful and well known financial institution of the region, and Marvin's father a powerful and well known figure of the governing board. It was his father's influence that convinced the Bank officials to hire him. Quick with numbers Marvin so far had earned a reputation as a good hand as a teller.

"We can wait Marvin."

"Yeah we can. But if we're gonna go let's go. We've gone over the prospect of this thing time without end."

"But how?"

J. T.'s only strategy centered on trying to talk some roadhouse into letting them play for pay until accumulating the necessary cash but adjudged that doing as much might not prove easy. Shortly however Marvin miraculously came up with an answer, joining J. T. in an air of dapperness and handed over a check in the amount of two hundred fifty dollars bearing the name of the New Mexico and Texas Cattle Association in the upper right hand corner, which he unwittingly failed to thoroughly examine. Even a peek at the erasing and cover up markings on the backside would have prompted alarm. "In retrospect I couldn't believe my gullibility, astonishing, and how terribly naïve I was to have followed his instructions."

"You take this check to the Farwell Bank of Commerce. They'll cash it. We're headin to Hollywood."

"Ha, ha, ha. You're something Marvin." I actually thought he'd conned his dad into giving him the check. After all, his signature appeared plainly on the face of it.

The small town of Farwell lay nine miles away, barely over the Texas border, to which J.T. carried the check, there having it cashed without incident, and returning to Clovis where hastily they threw together some packings and stationed themselves along route sixty six leading to Hollywood. They hitchhiked, and good luck seemed to have flown their way, a Hayes truck driver supplying a lift over the full distance, even buying their meals twice. The sudden jump to Hollywood was regarded as a touch of mild insanity by their friends who learned of it back home, but in actuality the undertaking made at least a particle of sense. A midget, George Havens, a close friend to J. T. for sometime already worked as a double for Little Beaver in the Red Rider series. George, a superb rider and stuntman relayed to him the most fascinating stories of the Hollywood stars and starlets and kept urging him to come on out.

"I'll gitchi a job J. T."

"At what?"

George proved his ability to deliver, persuading the director to let J. T. and Marvin do back ups in a posse scene, the job calling by union standards for a rate of pay of $37 per day, not bad for insignificant extras. But it only lasted for three days, and as valiantly as George tried he met with no success at landing them another, and so on his own J. T. began to search, accepting the first employment that availed itself, that of a singing telegram boy. Translated, this meant he went here and there in the city on a bicycle delivering messages by way of his singing them to the recipient, which to him seemed a veritable novelty and equally as hilarious. But this too played out — it very suddenly played out — and J. T. almost with it.

"I carelessly allowed my bicycle to swerve wildly against the edge of a run of streetcar tracks, which threw me heels over head into the pathway of a trolley. I could hear it coming. But I couldn't do anything to save myself. Not then. The jolt temporally knocked the breath out of me. As I say, I could hear it coming. I could hear the blaring of what seemed to be a foghorn, a warning. But I don't think the engineer could see me clearly. Or anything. It was too foggy, the reason I misjudged with my bicycle. Anyway, I roused myself to where in the nick of time I rolled over and away to safety. It's a stunning thing, I remember thinking, that one's existence can be so suddenly snuffed out. As quick as a flash. Here one second, gone the next. At times I still tremble when I think of such a close call."

Their stay in California was doomed from the ill conceived beginning. Without issue or debate in his own mind he rounded up Marvin and the both of them promptly devised plans for their return to Clovis, hitchhiking, J. T. anxious to get back but impervious to the dire news waiting at the end of the line. Before they reached Clovis Marvin's father settled matters with the bank at Farwell and the cattleman's association for his son's forgery, gravely advising his son when he saw him that the penitentiary quite properly dealt with those who wrongfully took other's possessions, usually severely. Marvin ultimately got around to sharing the story with J. T. which struck with an impact. "Lord help. What if my father learns of this?" It would not reach his father. Without hesitation he considered himself as guilty as Marvin, yet was never confronted by the authorities, strongly suspecting that his friend Marvin argued his case with his own father, effectively convincing him that he, J. T., three or four years his junior could only be guilty of youthful gullibility. As time ran on he began playing and singing again at Medley's Lounge, renewed of energy and freshness after laying off for a spell, but missing Ace who had become to his players and fans across the plains a living monument. Most people loved Ace and his rugged crude gut bucket singing too, which aptly conveyed who he actually was. The band reorganized without him under a new band leader after he said thank you but no more, —J. T. now the lead singer, and could have been the band leader, except he preferred the role as the number one singer and shunned the offer. For awhile he had occupied the lead guitar position but gave that up too. And that exactly suited him. He only wanted to sing. And since fans knew him far and wide as the star of the show his nightly presence without fail was imperative to Elcho, the owner, who mildly objected to his taking leave.

"You want off for a few gigs. Man, that's a hard one. You're the star J. T. You pack them in. You're putting me in a position to lose a bunch of money."

"The others sing too Elcho. They'd do all right filling in until I get on back."

"You've been singing here more than awhile and it's hard to turn you down. I remember when old Ace first brought you here. I hope you'll stay with me as long as he did, I mean off and on as long as he did."

J. T. remembered. They'd just left Elida, removing themselves from the desert to more desert, the latter not much of an improvement except that Santa Rosa could claim several times the population that resided in the boundaries of Elida and the Blue Hole beckoned nearby. But the character of the desert posed troubles for his psyche; he discovered earlier that he could not quite adapt to it, the imponderable expanse, the vastness, stretching on and on, and the constancy of the wind and dust too much for him to stand except for a limited while, yet these undesirables he did not give as the reason for asking for leave.

"It's my father and mother Elcho. We won't be getting back there anytime soon with the band and —."

"All right. That's a good enough reason. How does a week sound?"

"Thanks Elcho. I knew you wouldn't let me down."

Elcho had approved, appearing glad to have done it, deeming it as something owed, but later events revealed that the visit amounted to what J. T. called a colossal mistake. Soon he wished he hadn't gone. His father from the start vehemently opposed his venturing into the climate of music, picking and singing to the roadhouse crowds, and knowledge of it upset him to a point of uncontrollable anger. Next morning, after his son's arrival at near midnight, he called him aside.

"Son I'm disappointed. Deeply." J. T. blinked, his pulse quickening.

"How's that dad?" he answered as deferentially as he knew how, not faking that he failed to understand what his father meant because he did understand.

"Son, I'm saying it like I have to. That guitar, and where you're hanging out, is taking you straight down the road to perdition."

"Oh dad!"

"I mean it," he shot back with a scowl. "You think I'm old fashioned. But I know what I'm talking about. You're going down the road to ruin."

J. T. tried to hold his ground. "Dad, I'm sure it seems bad to you. And I do see some things I'd rather not. But I handle it. I'm a Christian. Nothing can change that."

In no mood to further talk his father began to turn away, his brow lifted, the sign of anger, with J. T. meekly trying to explain that all he aspired to do was sometime to land a recording contract, adding, but without making a dent that he always exerted his best to present himself as a role model for the musical people close around him — not drinking, not swearing, not messing around with questionable women — -going overboard to influence the young ones trying to break through, and honor the Lord as best he could too. But still his father stayed rigidly frozen, now edging away, his face fixed narrowly on the floor in disgust. His son was head strong and wouldn't listen, J. T. imagined his father thinking, and it crashed hard upon him.

"It'll be all right son." His mother who overheard from another room crept silently in and now pressed her hand softly to his arm. "You'll see. He has to let it sink in. Try to understand him. It's just his way."

"Ah."

"Please."

"Ah, how can I do that? It's not in me. His idea of worship is to rise on Sunday morning, read the Bible, and then attend church, and witness if asked, and he usually is, and then after that go to a campground gathering if there is one where they eat and carry on all day with gospel singing. I don't like gospel singing. I like country and western singing. And there's nothing wrong with that."

She gave no answer of agreement or disagreement, only, "You're a young man who's mindful of the Lord. He doesn't doubt that, not in his heart he doesn't. Give him time. He'll swing around."

"I am mindful of the Lord mom. I am all the time. And I read the Bible, sometimes after a show ending way after midnight. You don't see me do it, but I do. And always on Sunday. Of course I know that doesn't mean I'm a Christian. I am though as much as anybody else."

"You read the Bible. I didn't know you did, not as much as you now tell me. That's good. What do you read?"

"The New Testament. It's easier to follow. Seems to be written for people like me. I read in the Old Testament some, about the Kings mainly, and Judges, and if I really start to feel like taking on something that puts my brain to a test I open the pages to Revelation. But I seldom get far. What terrifying scary images. And who could understand their meaning?"

"Ah, you're a scholar son. Or else on your way to being one. I'm proud of you. Now, what are you to do about your father?"

"I think mom I'd better head on back to Santa Rosa. He needs to cool off and if I stayed around we'd have another butting of heads and that would only cause greater stress on you. And I don't want that even a little bit."

As all good mothers she took him into her arms, saddened at his going, wise in surmising that the possibility of another choice did not exist. If he left presently he would reach Santa Rosa in late afternoon, in time to see the quivering patches of sun light grow fainter and fainter and little by little slide below the rim of the great western plains.

With hurt in his heart he left, a troubling journey ahead, in that for every mile his father's voice echoed a condemnation of the profession he had chosen, and persistently he asked: "Was I foolish to go against him? Is this a crazy dream that I chase? Is it a waste, a dead end? Why can he not trust me, support me?" No longer would his father's home be his home, their views too acutely apart and making this more so was his age, a man now, when decisions concerning his future must be made by himself, rightly or wrongly, wise or unwise. In his heart he hoped and believed that someday his father would think of him proudly but still, sadly he had reached that definite milestone; he could not go home again. It persevered, and to help ease the pain he then or in a later moment of idleness sat down and put his thoughts in script,

I dream sometimes that I am there
At the place where I was born
I walk the fields on my father's heels
As he plows the growing corn

Precious are the memories
Of boyhood scenes back then
But they live only in my mind
You can't go home again,

stopping there, declining ever to write the finish, tucking the lines away in an old shoe box for safe keeping. He once admitted to Erskine in chat that it possibly might have made a pretty good song.

Shortly after retuning to Santa Rosa the sky seemed to open up with a long awaited opportunity when Jimmy Laredo, not his real name, came searching for a singer and guitar player who could be a major addition to his act. Already he recruited two exceptional musicians in Smoky and Dusty Coats, who J. T. already knew well, and was bound for Santa Fe, New Mexico to fill a booking at the highly touted Emile's Club. When Jimmy told him of the amount of pay he'd receive he tingled with excitement, and said with virtual certainty he'd take the job, but for a reason in addition to the size of the paycheck. Jimmy presently recorded with Columbia Records out of Los Angeles and J. T. calculated that to tie in with him might in someway help him secure a recording contract himself on down the line. And then he consulted with Elcho. "I don't blame you J. T. Take it. He can help boost your career. I cain't." They left the next day in Jimmy's dated but shiny, well kept, 1937 Packard, the exterior painted a high gloss blue, and engraved on the doors, left and right, were the letters in bold face print, Jimmy Laredo, his last name starting with the letter L thrice size normal.

"It ain't Laredo actually," said Dusty Coats to J. T. when they were reducing their biological accumulations at the very first rest stop. "It's Lawson. He invented the name Laredo with the notion it might make him more marketable than his real name. It does sound catchy, don't you think?"

"I think maybe it does."

Emile's came as a stunning surprise. Sheik and sophisticated, a few obvious steps up on Medley's Lounge with well financed superior management, the club attracted huge fun loving crowds, demonstratively appreciative of the band and the songs that Jimmy and J. T. selected and sang. They ate well. They slept well. Life was good. Surely his father would have approved. He wished they could stay forever but that wasn't to be. Within weeks they embarked on a whirlwind road trip — to promote Jimmy's record — playing in San Angelo, Texas, Lansing, Michigan, Decatur, Illinois, Sioux City, Iowa, and Saint Louis, Missouri. J. T. prayed that Jimmy's groaning old Packard would hold out and doubted that it might. Excessively heavy, the traveling gear occupied every available inch, inside and out, the most obvious being a casket shaped stand up guitar case strapped to the top of the car. No one ever knew among the members of the band whether or not the State of Illinois trooper on the motorcycle intended it as a prank when he pulled them over to check their equipage. What happened wasn't serious; only comedic. "What you boys got there, a body?" As J. T. unbuckled the tie straps and opened the lid to the encasement the trooper peeped cautiously inside. "Okay, go ahead." The band saved their guffaws for later, while someone quipped that the officer perhaps suspected that he might catch a carload of roughnecks half intoxicated, which drew instant inflammations from Jimmy. "Boys, let me tell you something. If that's so the man wasted his time. We're not roughnecks. Not in the least. We don't drink. We're class, down to the last man." The praising moved J. T., the words touching his heart, and suddenly he felt proud to be a part of a man endowed with standards so lofty, telling him so to his face, but went on with a minor correction, this being that he was a tad wrong about the drinking matter, that some of the band were known to take a sip now and then, including himself. "Aw, you mean socializing. That's not what I call drinking J. T. Drinking is when a man over does it, gets soppy drunk and goes so far as to abuse his family, his children. I've seen plenty of drinkers. Not a pretty sight. I take a dim view of a man like that. It's a funny thing. They say that raging rivers start with a tiny drop. That's the same with drinking. A nip turns into a sip and a sip into a sure enough drink and after that a guzzle. I know you. You don't drink. You're a good boy, a fine boy they told me before I picked you up at Medley's Lounge. Elcho said you're the best."

Their meandering across country finally ended; it ended in Nashville where Jimmy checked in with Columbia Records, the visit having to do with a recording session scheduled for the Tulane Hotel studio, the site where Francis Craig a popular big band leader of that period also recorded and J. T. knew of him. His hit tune *Near You* had sounded across the airways for months. They were recording that day in the morning hour ahead of Jimmy's session and J. T. sat in the gallery and watched and listened. The band, fifteen members strong, were smartly clad in show time clothing, black pants and red jackets, even for a recording session, the several brass instruments filling the dimly lit room with a reflection of glitter while he sat and salivated and wished in fantasy that he could be asked to play rhythm guitar for them. The next best thing was to have the famous band leader and singer autograph his highly rated record but before he could make his way to him the man slipped out the back doorway.

"It amazed me that I played so well on Jimmy's session Erskine, as I think I've mentioned to you one time or another. I wasn't as sharp as I thought I ought to have been cause up until I caught on with Jimmy I hadn't played much, only singing, only that, and second, it was taking something like a year for my index finger to heal which I injured while chopping meat in a grocery store."

"Chopping meat? I'd forgotten."

"Yeah. I worked part time. Elcho didn't have any objection. My bad finger was the main reason I gave up the lead guitar position. I'd tried to make a come back but the finger refused to heal the way I'd hoped. In time it did heal and through really aggressive practice I began to return to my former self, improving rapidly from there on."

"Did you go back to playing lead guitar?"

"No I didn't. I'd left Elcho by several months. But even if I had remained with him I wouldn't have asked to be restored to my former position. It wouldn't have been treating the guy right who earned the lead position over time and through sweaty sacrifice. But I did start playing lead for Jimmy when he took me on. After we'd finished with him in the studio that day I smilingly looked down at the scar and raised my hand and kissed my finger for getting well, realizing that this moment, my first time to play on a big time recording session, could have eluded me. It earned me fifty dollars and put a plus on my reputation. "

Though intending to stay with Jimmy for an indefinite length Smoky and Dusty and J. T. were compelled to seek work on their own while he busied himself promoting his record around Nashville, the interval that he would take unclear to him and to the record people, and while Jimmy acted with caution not to string them along he still spoke encouragingly.

"We'll get going pretty soon boys. In the meantime just pick up anything to earn yourselves some cash. I don't think I'll take long."

It would take forever. No consistent work could be found, so they ended up in San Angelo, Texas playing at the Wigwam Club and parading as a trio on station KTXL under the name The Sons Of The Prairie, a glaring resemblance to the popular cowboy movie singers of Hollywood fame, Sons of the Pioneers, an encroachment, clearly, yet no one bothered to complain. The contract at the Wigwam Club called for six months of work, longer than any that J. T. remembered and said as much to the Coats brothers, all three beginning to elaborate profusely on the good things coming their way. J.T. called Jimmy, thanking him for all he'd done for them, but relaying that they were happy with their current state of affairs and had opted not to rejoin him. As J.T. knew he would Jimmy accepted the news graciously, wishing them well.

"Good luck J. T. If I can at anytime in the future be of help to you and the guys let me hear from you."

"That's kind of you Jimmy. I will. And good luck to you too."

It was at the Wigwam Club restaurant, not the club, that he met Jennifer Hastings, Jen they called her, a quite beautiful young woman apparently, from whom there sprang an immediate arresting radiance and she swept into J. T.'s life likened to a thunderbolt as he put it. "As I entered the dining room my eyes fell arrestingly on the girl sitting behind the cash register. 'My Heaven, she's beautiful. There could not be another on earth to match her.' I must have smiled because she smiled too. I don't know for sure who did it first. Me, I suppose. But I know this. My heart melted faster than butter, and I almost forgot my whereabouts. Within five minutes I was to return to the stage in the adjoining room. During the next set I foggily went through my routines, my concentration veering uncontrollably off from where it ought to have been. All I could think of was that beautiful girl in the next room, hoping she'd be there when the session ended. She was. She worked the late shift. Maybe there was too much natural gall within me, but all the same I went up to her and introduced myself and she gave me her name too. It was instant affinity. From there on we literally could not stay away from one another. I started going to the restaurant every evening for dinner and she started coming to the club for the late show. That's the way it commenced Erskine. I've told it exactly."

"She must have been a pretty thing."

"Uh, huh, huh, huh. To say that young men, as well as the old, drew a deep breath on letting their eyes fall across her form and face is not in any way strong enough. You would have had to see her in full, her physical and sensual qualities, in addition to her natural beauty, to understand the strength of her appeal to the opposite gender. Tall and slender and skin kind of ivory white she qualified with ease as the perfect picture for a magazine cover."

"She was something I'm sure. I can see her now. You must have doubted your senses. In this context I'm facetiously drawn to Adam in Milton's *Paradise Lost,* dreaming that Eve was a mere illusory figment of his own conjuring but on awakening discovered her to be actually real."

"Ha, ha, ha. Something likened to that. But Jenny was real all right. Eventually the club management recognized her beauty and decided to act on it, at first not knowing exactly what to do with her but they figured out, presenting her as a flower girl that handed out roses to the gentlemen guests who sought the adornment for pinning to the lapel of their female companions. She took on her new job the third week after I met her, earning triple the amount she earned working the cash register, not to mention tips. The crowds swarmed to the club just to see her, men and women. She had to be aware of her charm, how could she not have been, fitting perfectly into the attire that management asked her to wear, nice sheik gowns or colorful blouses and skirts; but opting to clad her in tight fitting jeans — though infrequently — and a pair of stylish little green bells affixed loosely to the boots on her feet that jingled up and down as she moved throughout the crowd. Everyone liked to call her Jenny Bell, though after the show resorted again to her usual name, Jen. They loved her either way. Things couldn't have gone better. She was in Heaven; we both were.

It was something of strangeness that I began to divine that a sort of charm lived within her , a symbol of good luck maybe, which actively transferred to me, and that soon I'd begin to move progressively toward a recording contract. It pretty well happened that way too, unexpected, as a good many record deals do. I don't mean that it happened absolutely instantly. I just mean that I sensed that it had begun to. But in the meanwhile I'd have to finish falling deeper in love with her, if possible. With heart and soul I adored her, and strove to be with her on every chance. How vividly I recall it all."

"Recall it all! You mean you have more to tell. I see! Go on. I like it."

"All right. Let me see. Oh yes. When catching odd times from our usual work place we'd avail ourselves to other nightspots, small dinky cafes, which she liked best, losing ourselves in some out of the way corner at a table lighted with candles flickering and quivering. We sat looking at one another in the misty glow, with me drowning in her soft gorgeous eyes. Her every detail enchanted me and I even studied the rise and fall of the pulsations in her neck and counted the repetitions. In my imagination and hope I lived inside her heart, that mysterious crypt of romance, and knew she in her fantasy lived in mine. We were everywhere together, two young people hopelessly infatuated with one another and in love. She had attained to age twenty and I to twenty three. We would marry. I sincerely uttered my vows, as sincerely as I ever avowed anything, just as she uttered hers. I wished my father and mother could have been there for the wedding. Ace Ball, dressed in a shiny new suit, drove down from Clovis to act as best man. At about this same time station KWTX in Waco offered me an opportunity to headline a show while also the Terrace Club in that city asked me to be the featured singer for their nightly events, Jenny and I at once talking it over. There could only be one obvious answer: her mother lived in Waco and she entertained an irrepressible wish to live near her; so I acted immediately to accept the two offers, regrettably saying goodbye to Dusty and Smoky. Things were going well, my pay good and Jenny happy to be near her mother. I thought our roots were planted for a long long while. But that would not be in the making. Hank Thompson, already under contract with Capitol Records, started to sing for a station in the city with an outreach much greater than mine, and was a very popular artist, his hit tune *Humpty Dumpty Heart* racing across the airwaves. I knew him from earlier show events that we did together. He began to sit in on my performances and I began to sit in on his and this led to our having lunch together, or coffee, and that led to something quite appetizing to my interest."

'Tell you what J. T. I'm moving to Dallas to headline the Big D Jamboree, and I want you to go with me to open the show. I realize it's a kind of imposition, a strain on Jenny, but I badly need you and I'm going to say something that I don't think you'll turn down.'

'What's that?'

'If you'll take me up on my proposal I'll promise as much as a man can promise to get you a recording deal.'

"I swallowed. And wasted no time saying yes. The Big D Jamboree loomed as a grand place to play. While tenfold the size of Sled Allen Arena in Lubbock it fell short of rivaling other greater venues, Nashville and The Louisiana Hayride, but in my thinking there was not a single qualm in regard to that. It made me ecstatic just to be there. At first I wasn't happy with the role they assigned me, The Traveling Texan: Masked Singer of Folk Songs — though I hurriedly adapted once viewing the size of my first pay check, along with hearing the rousing acclaim of the crowds. All sorts of oddities popped up during the show, unpredictable, as you might imagine, which the crowd enjoyed as well as myself, but an incident took place off stage soon after I started to work that I found difficult to appreciate. I'm taking it that you'd like to hear a shortened version."

"I'll bet I will."

"Yeah. Once I got stopped by the security police assigned to the show. I'd arrived early wearing my outfit. They hadn't yet learned of the act. When someone explained that the mask was merely part of my attire on stage they let me go and practically burst open with laughter. It didn't seem so funny to me. I might have been the victim of a bullet. I guess a year passed when Hank signed on with KSKY radio in Dallas and as it was with the Big D Jamboree asked me to join him to open the show, singing a couple or more numbers. As he said they would our voices reached over a sizeable distance, both of us gaining tremendously in popularity and recognition. One day unexpectedly he dropped into my dressing room with the sweetest news that ever came to my ears.

'J. T. your time is here. Capitol Records is going to sign you.'

'Wha, what did you say?'

'A record deal. You have a record deal that's on its way.'

My throat went numb. I could not fathom the message that seemed astoundingly unreal. For a moment an indescribable drunken happiness seized me. After the jolt subsided a little I thanked him more than amply, shaking his hand up and down until he necessarily pulled it away. "

"Well I'll be. You made it"

"Yep, Erskine, old 1949, a year impossible to forget and I can't forget Hank either. He kept his promise. And I could go on to stress that on the one hand the road to a record deal had ended but in the reality of the matter it had only started — granted, the pay better, the venues grander, the recognition stunning, and the rubbing of shoulders with the elite of the recording industry muchly satisfying but still there was the ceaseless energy draining travel that you couldn't duck. It would be the same old road in many respects that you'd traveled without let up year after year in the past, the food you ate not the best for you and that goes for staying up late at night. Being an artist is hard work and I found that stardom made it harder, not easier. "

"But you also experienced some good moments."

"Can't say otherwise. There were many wonderful moments. Signing the contract one of them for sure. Also, joining with Ace Ball at the Sled Allen Arena and a bunch of other venues, roadhouse crowds and all. Yep, I recall my experience with Ace as one of the rare ventures of my life and my tenure as well with Elcho at Medley's Lounge in Santa Rosa. And I don't forget Eldon Shamblin, not for a second I don't. If a young man, a beginner, asked me what it's like to go through the sacrifices necessary for earning his way into the music business I'd tell him the truth, that it's hard as hell but the outcome justifies the pain. These young adventurers won't stop climbing for the big time no matter how terrifically they get knocked down. You can see them every day pouring into the cities with their guitars strapped across their backs; and at night sleeping in greyhound bus stations, or on the hard wooden benches in the city parks. The yearning to reach the top is a mighty force in a young human being. I feel for them. I deeply do. But I have to confess that if I'm gonna feel sorry for anybody it's the old timers, the old artists whose days are spent, whose age has put them in a rocking chair with not enough means to care for themselves. They wasted their money. Sad. Why they did that and why they keep doing that I don't know, unless it's their philosophy of life that does it, which is that tomorrow doesn't matter, live it up today, there's no need to hold on to anything for very long.

The thing I regret most as I look back is what my wonderful Jenny had to put up with. I didn't blow money, I didn't drink, and I didn't mess around with the women — there being a ton of them to mess around with — but as constantly as a steady drummer's beat the road forever beckoned and since she seldom traveled with me she endured an unfair share of sitting at home and waiting and worrying. She meant everything to me, and when she died several years ago, childless, as I have told you, I almost died with her. But with the scriptures at my side and the Good Lord helping I made it back to sanity."

"Was your mother still living then?"

"She was. She came to stay with me for awhile, a sustaining rock as mothers are and quite frankly went a long way toward pulling me through. My father passed away a few years before that, not many, and we had largely reconciled our differences, but not altogether. I hated it that we hadn't.

Well that's about it Erskine. Our life is simple now, yours and mine, living in this big city in fine houses next to one another, way back off from the heavy traffic, not ever going anywhere much or needing to, just delighting ourselves for the most part talking to one another of old times and every once in a while weaving in a word or two of our favorite topic, the ups and downs of the hard road that leads to a record deal. Correct me if I'm wrong but I don't think I've ever once said I wouldn't travel it again if I could roll back some years and start all over."

The Strangest Marriage

"IT WAS the strangest marriage, the strangest that I ever ran across in my practice of the law," said Mister J. H. Puryear, my mentor in the large prestigious law firm that I joined as an intern a little better than twelve months ago. Of Jewish heritage Mister Puryear migrated to the American shores from European Bavaria when a boy, starting in the not too many years ahead to study law and after graduating joined the very law firm in this sprawling city where now I am myself employed. Lucky for me that I landed a post as a trainee under his counsel and direction, by far the oldest and wisest man in the firm, with numerous cases of record which he won and I considered myself to be fortunate in the extreme to have him at my side. He treated me most gently and made every effort where need be to help me with legal complexities that were at times confounding and virtually beyond my grasp. He was then seventy years of age, or past. He called me Jacob, a sort of nick name, his choice for the reason he never got around to explaining. He allowed me generous latitude when I visited him for a sit, encouraging an expression of thoughts and questions that came to me from time to time. But I employed caution not to over do saying or asking him anything, too busy listening, recognizing my opportunity, an opportunity to listen and learn. An attractive young woman a few years beyond my age, an intern as well, occupied an office next to mine, exceedingly quick in the field of law and by some measure slightly ahead of me. We often talked and she did her best to lend assistance. But I believe we were equally good for one another. Mister Puryear especially encouraged us to collaborate as a team. He held a particular fondness for her, I think, because she showed no hesitancy to speak out on subjects of issue. Above her office door the letters Olga Leporte appeared. I called her Olga and Mr. Puryear called her Leporte. Sometimes she joined us, at lunch as a rule, and it especially pleased me that she did because she raised many interesting and pertinent questions and I learned from the answers that Mister Puryear appeared happy to provide.

Twice each week I went with him from our office to a dinge for lunch that bore the appellation Sidewinder, the business name, situated just off a cobblestone back street, a niche bulging with a heavy counting of his old contemporaries who spoke to him most affably as we entered, some rising in deference. As a rule, after we ordered, the two of us sitting alone and undisturbed, he would take up a topic for discussion, which he selected from an array of potentials, and would go over it in exhaustive detail. It was the same on this day. But Olga would not join us just yet, though invited. She would catch up later.

"Well Jacob, what shall we talk about, murder, bribery, theft, insider trading, fraudulent land claims, scandal, embezzlement, which?"

"I'm not sure sir. But I'm certain they're all enticing and that I will be greatly benefited to learn from either, whichever it is."

"Well all right. Today, I'll surprise you. Allow me my fine young friend to take up a conflict of wills, which I choose to reference as the strangest marriage — because it indeed could not be seen otherwise once you familiarized yourself with its rocky vicissitudes and that it was destined from the beginning to end in a bitterly fought divorce. Mind you. You are to butt in at any time you feel like it."

And so he began.

"Let me step back a little if I may. It's a story of an ill fated marriage and a subsequent divorce all right, but it is also about child custody which quickly came into play and became prominent. That's key. Mark it down. Divorce is common as far as marriages go, as you know, yet the charges and counter charges in this case were not in any respect common, and cannot, and will not, be considered as anything but rare once the components of the tumultuous drama are set in place and inspected.

The husband and wife were married in the spring of 1970, living throughout the union with the husband's mother, who in my opinion was partially if not greatly at fault. The couple's relationship starting to deteriorate a very short while following the utterance of wedding vows. The wife felt that the husband and mother were controlling and oppressive, the husband alleging the wife unfit. Even so, a child was born from the marriage; but we are not to be caught off guard in learning that in October, 1972, the wife filed petition for divorce and eventually the court ruled to grant it on grounds of inappropriate marital conduct by the husband and designated her as the primary residential parent of the party's child, further ruling that the wife deserved to be awarded a portion of her attorney's fees and discretionary fees which the husband would be compelled to pay. The husband pled to the appellate court of the state for a reversal. With an exception or two they quickly sided with the trial court and remanded the major part of the issues back to that jurisdiction for ruling. "

"Stating it to be your opinion you said sir that the mother of the husband appeared largely at fault for the breakdown of the marriage. What makes you feel that way?"

"The reasons surfaced in the trial. I attended as a mere spectator as much as I could. I had driven down from the city here to represent a client, a corporation, in a land dispute in the area where the trial was docketed. As luck would have it I dropped into the courtroom as things were getting underway. I often sat in on trial court arguments, sometimes only to observe the opposing lawyers do battle, and I sat in on this proceeding quite often, once I sniffed the nature of it, and subsequently read the transcript of record from beginning to end. You should learn to do that as well. Your question will be answered soon enough pursuant to the mother in law ganging up on the girl with her son. I will now retell what the court said and adjudged, and can do it well, in any event with miniscule variation, for, as I more or less indicated, I sat through the bulk of the sessions and have read the recordings three or more times. 'This is a tortuous saga of an ill fated marriage," they wrote, and got directly into the fact that Tracy Delaney and his mother Martha Ann Delaney had lived in Fort Worth, Texas for awhile and that they ran a successful bridal and tuxedo enterprise together with a jewelry business in a refurbished shopping center dotted with an assortment of antique shops. They had taken an unpretentious declining building and converted it into the Delaney Fashion Center. At church in late fall of 1969 Tracy met Yvonne Warner who then worked at multiple jobs, one as a clerk in a department store and another as a part time baby sitter. At this phase of his life Tracy had attained to forty two years of age, Yvonne then age twenty three years, Tracy therefore within four years of doubling the age of his future wife." He stopped briefly and

I took advantage of the interlude to comment on a fragment or two that particularly caught my attention.

"Which suggests immaturity on the part of the girl, the age suggesting it I mean to say, and foolish of a man long seasoned by age and experience to be pursuing her. Shouldn't he have known better even if she didn't?"

"Ha. It would seem so. But the way of a man's heart can be gravely error prone in the face of beauty, youth, and lure, irrespective of the weight of years on his shoulders. But let us see into that as we journey on," Mr. Puryear answered with detachment. "And oh yes Jacob. I haven't yet mentioned that neither were ever married before. And while they were dating, let me squeeze in, Tracy and Yvonne studied the Bible together and went over their religious beliefs at length, while at other sittings Yvonne entered into a great many like discussions with her future mother in law as well; and soon, wouldn't you know it, Yvonne left her present employment in favor of working for her future mother in law at the Delaney Fashion Center. It required but a pittance of time for Yvonne and Tracy to elect to marry. Just as the goddess of ill omen in long ago antiquity presided over marriages destined to split asunder, which tales of old speak of, she surely presided over theirs. The court pretty well said the same thing, calling it an ill fated marriage. In any event Tracy and Yvonne agreed jointly, according to wording from the trial court's record, that Yvonne as the dutiful wife would assume the role as full time homemaker and prepare to raise the children they hoped to have. It soon leaked out that Yvonne was in a strained relationship with her family with whom she resided, her parents objecting to her closeness with Tracy, harboring misgivings of the association to say the least, and alleged that he and his mother were intermixed with a cult, or appeared to be cultish, whereas, infuriated when she told him of such views Tracy promptly encouraged, perhaps precipitously encouraged, her to move from her parents home, and that she should tell them that they must admit lying about him and repent what they said, or else she would sever her affiliation with them once and for all — and at that intermission Yvonne decided to have no further contact with her family, moving to accommodations furnished by Tracy and his mother. It is unclear whether these accommodations were at his home, but whether they were or were not, it became so that his mother, Martha Ann Delaney, assumed the position as Yvonne's surrogate mother and assured her that she had just left a dwelling of the cursed and now resided in a place of the blessed. In April of 1970 Tracy and Yvonne tied the knot in a lavish ceremony performed by an ordained minister but I have observed that the couple did not obtain a marriage license from the state because Tracy contended a license to be unnecessary and would only result or might result in the state's interference with his private life; so therefore, their marriage fulfilled the description of a common law marriage, recognized in the state where they lived. The honeymoon over, Tracy, Yvonne perhaps expecting the contrary but not fussing, opted not to move from his mother's house, and it doubtless augured in his reckoning that there he and his new wife were settling down permanently. On the outset Yvonne received instructions or learned by some other conveyance that she must perform, as a family obligation, a list of duties in the home, Tracy having asked his mother in advance to mentor her in the performance of these duties — cooking, laundering, ironing his shirts, polishing his shoes, and notwithstanding, supplying guidance and direction in womanly arts, such arts embracing the finery of embroidery, pretty hand writing and calligraphy, and even the principles of Christian thought and behavior."

"Could you pause here sir? Christian thought and behavior! Seems somebody figured she wasn't measuring up to their self proclaimed standards; so they'd retrain her."

"Something like that."

"But while they were courting and reading the Bible together it seems to me that her lack of Christian principles should have been then apparent and if they were then Mister Delaney should have turned and gone away. Seems to me that he and his mother were setting themselves up on a lofty high plain and that she in their opinion hadn't attained to that height and so they'd see to it that she did. That's the darndest thing I ever heard. Husband suddenly telling his wife he's going to teach her the correct morals and Christian principles. Screwy! Suppose she had turned the tables on him."

"Turned the tables on him?"

"Yes sir. And why not? Suppose she had insisted that it should be her code by which they should live, not his, and insisted on schooling him accordingly."

"A good analogy Jacob and I wondered along the same course of reasoning. Anything else?"

"Not now."

"Well, let's see, oh yes. Given this background it is in no manner surprising that the bonds between the husband and wife began to seriously weaken, the husband beginning to complain of his wife's performance of household duties; and right away starting to keep a journal in which he recorded his observation of her behavior, focusing on things which he deemed unsatisfactory. Among other criticisms, he wrote that she became increasingly angry, ungodly, untruthful, and emotionally unstable, prone to what he termed 'tantrums.'"

"That's when she ought to have said 'goodbye buster boy,' but she didn't."

"No she didn't. I can't imagine keeping a journal on my wife. Wouldn't that be something? She'd oust me on my head in fifteen seconds once she found out. Anyway, the drama only expanded, got more entangled.

Yvonne showed up pregnant in June, shortly after their marriage, and received no medical consultation until late September or October, at which time Martha Ann arranged for a midwife, a Francis Selma, to conduct an examination. Despite Selma's request to meet privately with the expectant mother for a verbal exchange the husband and his mother insisted on their presence at the meeting, as well as at the physical examination. During this first and other visits Yvonne's demeanor was meek and quiet and virtually all questions were asked by Martha Ann and Tracy. From here, the schism between Yvonne and her mother in law did not narrow but widened, spawned from hours of Martha Ann's drillings and cutting disapprovals. And Tracy matched his mother's tactics. And all this stacked up layer after layer into the psyche of the new wife. No wonder her mood and confidence spiraled downward. To appease them, Yvonne made attempts to perform in compliance with their expectations, but invariably failing, which led to episodes of despair, and self loathing — and "self mutilation, scratching her face," Tracy attested in court — as well as anger, in protest of the constraints; and this led to further disapproval from the husband and his mother, to which Yvonne, lamb like, responded with remorse, supplication, and pleas for forgiveness of transgressions, and for help in attaining to the expected standards. As part of these deference's, most pitiable by any regard, she, at her husband's direction spent an entire month in the company of her mother in law devising and crafting a code of conduct termed Sixteen Promises by which she agreed to live. All sixteen were made record of at the proceedings of the trial court but only a part of the whole I shall here recite, having retained but a fragment of the others. But it is of both, those that I remember well and those that I do not concisely remember that I look upon with an emotion of comedy and laughter, laughing because the whole exercise was so comedic as to be absurd — and therefore I must laugh. It appeared that the mother-in-law transitioned into the likeness of a first grade teacher teaching principles of loyalty to the nation's youth. "

"And those that you said you remember were, were — ."

"To be sure I am getting to that. They were:

'I will stand tall to my calling to be Tracy's godly help mate and keeper of the home.

I will be in right relationship with family members, showing proper respect and honor.

I will maintain a selfless submissive attitude in all family relationships.

I will receive correction gladly when corrected at a task, and will not exaggerate the mistake by adding unrelated generalizations.

I will be obedient.

I will not be an emotional woman, led by a deceived heart.'"

"A perfect script for ego building," I rendered in satire. My dear friend let fly with laughter that receded to the far side of the room, drawing looks from patrons that conveyed what they and I both knew that Mr. Puryear seldom laughed as loudly, and that something just said traversed effectively to the quick of his pleasure center.

And when he quieted: "Each of the Sixteen Promises was followed by numerous scripture quotations, Jacob, and as an addenda to this Yvonne was directed or forced to memorize and recite the Promises, as well as Biblical passages relating to the behavior standards set down for her to meet. Tracy's rather bizarre journaling during these episodes, as presented in court, reflects vividly his disapproval of her performance of domestic tasks such as cleaning and cooking, her failure to complete an elaborate scrapbook of their honeymoon, and her clumsiness with a baby doll used as a practice object in baby care while waiting for arrival of the day of birth.

And the journal further evinces his reproaches for his wife's comments which reflected either anger at the disapproval from him and Martha Ann or self hatred for not meeting expectations. At or about this time, the reason escaping me, the mid wife Selma moved from the area and Martha Ann secured a replacement, an Ester Traywick, who examined Yvonne in January of 1971, and the same as with Selma, this and other sessions with Yvonne were closely accompanied by Tracy and Martha Ann. In late spring the child was born, Connie Ann Delaney they named her, a home birth, with Traywick attending. During this procedure Yvonne received no anesthetic in that Tracy and his mother persuaded her to agree to a natural childbirth. And moreover, prior to the birth, Tracy decided that he did not want a birth certificate to be issued by the state, citing the probability of government interference with his family, having his way but only partially, for Traywick, the midwife, tricked him, in short time filing a birth certificate of sorts for the child, giving only the child's last name, the date of birth, the city and county of the birth, where the birth occurred — the street address — the name of the attendant and the mother's first name, Yvonne, and the father's full name, Tracy Delaney. Aside from his quirkiness at filing a certificate of birth he behaved in an equal extreme by denying the baby's examination by a pediatrician as well as declining to have her immunized.

The husband and his mother went on operating their business, spending the usual hours at Delaney Fashion Center, leaving Yvonne at home to care for the newborn. A peek at the husband's journal entries would have uncloaked a rash of criticisms of his wife's parenting skills, housekeeping efforts, failure to do expected assignments, and of her continued cycle of emotional behaviors, alternating, he said, from pleas for forgiveness of shortcomings and earnestly praying with her mother in law in which she dedicated herself to being born again, to episodes of anger, self loathing, and self mutilation. In the summer that followed another disturbance erupted, perhaps related to the other criticisms, but yet different. The father, concluding he'd tolerated enough, suddenly ended sexual relations, admitting in his journal that he asked his wife to sleep in the guest room in that he feared her violent temper. Even despite this low ebb in their affiliation the husband hadn't given up in his struggle to rehabilitate his wife, meeting with his mother to formulate and post a document at some conspicuous location in the home entitled Our 16 Rules by Which We Live, which they went over with Yvonne, point by point, with Yvonne acceding to memorize and be able to recite on call the wording of each stricture and abide at all times by them. As if this were not enough Tracy took to making red notations on a calendar when Yvonne would have a temper tantrum as he termed it, and this was followed by the mother in law counseling her daughter in law long into the night. Completely lacking, it seems to me, was the father's sensitivity, or even having knowledge of such a thing, to the powerful maternal instinct that lives in a mother's breast for her child and it struck me amazingly when I read in his own words his complaints that the baby was the sole object of the mother's affection — why in the hell wouldn't she have been — and that she attempted to get the baby's attention while he held it in his arms; going on from there to levy his disapproval of the mother's excessive and sensual kisses and inappropriate stroking of the baby as well as the mother's protest at being excluded from caring for her. There rose a swell of pity in my heart when I further read that Yvonne had been persuaded or by her own choice, severely influenced by daily brainwashing I supposed, to write an apology to Martha Ann in repentance, promising never again to rub the baby or 'fawn over her,' or say 'Mommy loves you' over and over again for that is weird."

Then Mister Puryear abruptly rose from his chair in quest of relieving his biological processes, "My age Jacob; when I have to go I have to go, sorry," then went on to the men's room, and after a brevity came out and made his way over to an old gentlemen, age eighty and better Mr. Puryear said, the two of them hugging and uttering endearments to one another while breaking into broad grins, and then he returned to our table.

"An old friend Jacob, indeed an old friend. For the longest I practiced law with him. We won many a suit together. Sorry to have cut out on you. Now, where were we?" he asked, rubbing his hands together as if pepped up to get back into the flow.

"It had to do with the son and his mother depriving Yvonne of the right and opportunity to show affection for her baby. How ridiculous! Somebody must have been nuts and I don't think it was Yvonne."

"Yeah. I concur with that."

"While you were gone I set in to thinking. How powerful the mother's maternal instinct. Human or animal. I read once that this is convincingly seen in the proud lioness that'll fight to the death to save her cubs from a marauder."

With a nod he showed agreement and said something of the fascinating truth of nature wherein that mother's of all species, whether animal or human, were alike in this regard and from there picked up again with his story.

"As the year 1972 approached the husband out of the blue started contemplating that the family should move to an isolated area of the country, with no reason given whatsoever Yvonne later corroborated, and in mid November 1971 he and his mother sold the business, the Delaney

Fashion Center, for over $1 million and promptly bought a house and farm in a rural area fifty miles north of Paducah, Kentucky for $275,000. The wife's name did not appear on the deed. The family, in other words the mother in law, the husband, and Yvonne and the baby moved into the house shortly after the deed allowed possession, a clap board two story dwelling needing work, and I seriously wonder how utterly bewildered Yvonne, a city girl born and raised, must have been at getting dragged several hundred miles away from her hometown to a rural countryside that could be reasonably described as the boondocks."

"It must have been jolting," I let out. "Naturally I don't know what went on inside her heart, but it's easy to imagine. Well, so there they were, way out in the middle of nowhere, with nothing to do apparently. I refer mainly to Tracy and Martha Ann. Of course they didn't have to do anything because they'd sold their business in Texas for over a million bucks."

"That could have been their view. But wasn't the way things would pan out. They couldn't see it creeping up but a specter had subtly started to move toward them that would significantly bite into their wealth. In the meanwhile, with the Delaney Fashion Center no longer a burden on their shoulders, eating up their time, they true enough could stay home during the day, and this must have meant the worst of misery for Yvonne, a supposition well born out, for the apparent one sided war of conflict grew still worse, the father more vigorously trumping up charges of Yvonne's disrespectfulness toward him and his mother and that she constantly upset the baby with her temper tantrums. The father's journaling in or about December 1971 stated that the mother of the child was asked to leave the main floor to think, pray, and rework her motives and life choices, and at that time there existed a complete separation. Tracy moved the mother into isolation by assigning her to a bedroom situated in the lower level of the house and forbade her to see her daughter. There, in her confinement the mother was required, I did say required, to work on her neutralizing projects, the nature of which involved the act of scripting apologies for errors toward her husband and his mother (writings long and elaborate) acknowledging alleged wrong doings on topics of varying content — the most eccentric centering on, 'How I Destroyed My Marriage.' Sometimes they were numerously copied and recopied, as commanded, and during this period the mother could not leave her space of confinement except to go to the bathroom, escorted, the husband bringing her meals to her, never allowing her to come to the kitchen or dining room. The writings were to no avail, the husband complained, and the mother therefore remained in isolation through Christmas during which Tracy denied her the opportunity to be with her daughter. And then, all at once the New Year came."

More than mildly it ran in my analysis that the treatment to which the Delaney's subjected Yvonne constituted torture and torment or both and likely would have resulted in the husband and mother in law serving time were their extraordinary cabals put before the court as specific charges above and beyond the ongoing suits. And I teetered on the edge of exclaiming as much. But held up, glad I did because Mr. Puryear would delve further into the drama shortly. My interruption, I feared, would lessen his concentration.

"Something Jacob?" he asked, his voice unraised, seeing apparently that I stood poised to jump in.

"No sir. Not just yet. It can wait."

"Okay. All right." And then —

"In the second week of 1972, while still in isolation in her bedroom Yvonne argued with Tracy upon his paying call, during which she accused him and his mother of conspiring to take her daughter away from her and asked if he ever wanted to have sexual relations with a woman again. Somehow he took this as a slight to his manhood, which might well have been so, and thus lunged into fury and determined then and there that she should be evicted from the house, and with no contact with her daughter ever again. Then he removed Yvonne from the main dwelling and quartered her in a tenant house on the grounds referred to as the Quiet Recluse used for the purpose of miscellaneous storages. The tenant house stood out of sight from the main house, with painted over windows that no one could see through or out of and worse still contained no hot water for any purpose. Compounding these strictures even more excessively Tracy decreed that in order to stay in the Quiet Recluse she would have to yield to yet more rules, ten of them, all in writing and accepted by signature, under which she would not be allowed to waste water, food, or electricity, nor to commit careless acts, nor to open the front or back door or answer if someone should knock, and could not leave the house for whatever the reason. She would sleep on a cot, with Tracy bringing her groceries twice a week, and during this interim forced to continue writing her neutralizing projects, and yet still permitted no contact with her daughter. I guess in the wake of all this Yvonne had had enough, likened to the straw that broke the camel's back, for in April, the records show, after not seeing her daughter since early December, she opted to write Tracy a letter asking him to allow her to move back into the family home so that she could see her child, and upon writing the letter left the Quiet Recluse to personally deliver it, though on ringing the door bell found no one home. So she slid it through the crack under the door. Seeing her leaving the Quiet Recluse as a violation of his previously set rule Tracy broke into rage and promptly scripted a lengthy draft entitled Provisions of Divorcement and Terms and Conditions Hereof. The next day he delivered the document to her, announcing on the spot his declaration of divorce and that she must leave. In the Provisions he purported that his action was taken devoid of court order, and could be, since they, he and Yvonne, were married without license of marriage from the state, therein describing contemporaneously his perception of her conduct and citing such conduct as a basis for his declaration. The Provisions were prefaced by numerous disparaging allusions to Yvonne's family, her lack of money, and his past exertions to benefit her and more."

"Could I cut in?"

I'd been aching to do as much ever since he mentioned that the girl was banished to the storage house, or even before. Pausing, he looked over kindly as if to suggest that I more than deserved an interval to speak and that he gladly yielded.

"Mr. Puryear, here this girl was far away from home, far away from anyone that could represent her cause, coldly exiled to an out house and denied being with her own flesh and blood child. That constituted grounds for charges of extreme cruelty and in my opinion those people, Tracy and his mother, deserved to end up in jail."

"You're asking me for my opinion in addition to yours?"

"Yes sir. I am."

"Then you shall have it. My opinion agrees with yours. They could have been prosecuted and found guilty and sentenced and punished severely. But no one prosecuted them for the offense of question. It wasn't up to the girl to do this. She had neither the knowledge nor the ability nor the grit nor the money. Those that could have done something, her legal counsel, didn't, perhaps irresponsibly letting the water pass on under the bridge without sticking a single finger into it. This is merely a speculation you understand."

"I do."

"Now, I happen to have with me in my little attaché case a copy of perhaps Tracy's most complete attack on his wife, as presented to the court, knowing that I would be sitting with you and realizing the contents were too lengthy for my recall and further knowing that you'd need to see them with your own eyes I have brought them along and now spread them before you."

It was of abbreviated length. I read every line from the first to the last, the exact words, I emphasize, from the hand of the husband Tracy Delaney.

"I offered to assist Yvonne with her difficulties and shortcomings even before our marriage. I asked my mother to begin the immense task of mentoring this woman. Hundreds of documented hours were spent teaching her on every topic imaginable — from homemaking, hygiene, kitchen prep and cooking, laundering, polishing, mothering, homemaking, to principles of Christian thought and behavior, practical work ethic, womanly art subjects such as embroidery, hand writing and calligraphy, and many more. This mentoring kindly continued throughout most of the period of our marriage. She began to display tendencies of unchristian behavior from the start and I began the immense task of trying to deal with her erratic sociopathic but worst of all violent behavior. A bizarre patchwork began to emerge of a person ungodly, vain, incredibly lazy, proud, massively self centered, double minded, angry, careless, babbling, unreasonable, scripture twisting, Laodicean, Phillistine, self indulgent, and juvenile who told multiple lies multiple times without a shred of conscience or remorse, bearing no resemblance to a woman of 25 years of age in her conduct or lifestyle and I began to document her behavior in diary form. During our early months her mentor, my mother, developed with her, her own code of ethics which she memorized. They became appropriately titled her Promises. Our 16 Rules by Which We Live she also memorized and in exact detail. These rules are in fact the codes by which we as a family are to abide. Although curiously able to recite these rules and many scriptural passages by heart, there was never a significant adoption of them in her behavior or lifestyle choices. The conscience of my wife has been totally seared and she is disastrously double minded and unstable in all her ways. By conservative estimates she has broken her own Promises, Our 16 Rules, the Ten Commandments, and her own word multiple times beyond the Biblical 70 x 7, even past several thousand times. I estimate 5,000 to 7,000 times. She does not serve the God of Abraham, Isaac, and Jacob as I do, and this is a clear case of unequal yoking. By early November she was released from all duties of normal family life and began to write her projects in her private bedroom. But this would not restrain her from over using her mouth, nor act in any way to match the family codes of behavior, codes she had memorized without flaw. She was asked to leave the marriage bed for the first of many times in December because of her grossly rebellious behavior and as of April of the next year this became the permanent arrangement, in as much as there was no change ever seen in her endless cycle of selfishness, foolishness, arguing, lying, and hateful violence. This constituted abandonment, beyond question, and adjoining this violation with her conduct of abuse, violence, deceit, and hatred formed the grounds for the complete separation and divorce of husband and wife."

There were other lambastings to his attack, equally as cutting, mixed with another aspect of his intentions, but I did not at that time go on to read these, concluding however that he had written them in a state of fervor as he had in the previous outpouring. I then turned back to Mr. Puryear.

"It's an eye full Jacob, I'm sure you'll agree."

I chortled. "Yes sir. Quite an eyeful. I'm amazed that he reared up with such voluminous condemnations. The tirade, absurd as it was, surely worked against him in the final judgments. "

"Indeed. I'm amazed that his lawyers used the material in their argument."

"I've read only the abbreviations here on paper. I guess I didn't need to read the full volume. But did he alter his disparagements to any detectable degree in the remainder?"

"Not much. But some. He wove them in where he thought he needed to. By and large he began to focus on rather specific plans for disposing of his marriage and laying out the terms to which his wife was to agree. Banking on his own pronouncements as scripted into his Provisions of Divorcement and Terms Hereof he began to go over what had to happen or would happen in order to divest himself of Yvonne, this being: first, that since there was no need to secure approval for marriage license, then so too there was no need to secure state approval for divorce; and second, that in kindness to his wife he was agreeing to graciously provide her with a one time lump sum of $2000 in final settlement in exchange for the complete execution of divorcement, and that this meant she was never again under any circumstances to enter into Kentucky or Texas to seek her child, nor send by proxy her representatives to these states; and third, that his wife was acknowledging her abuse of her infant child and family, the repeated violation of her adopted family codes, her violence, her insane envy, her continual breaking of the Ten Commandments, and then here he goes again, her massive lying, her selfish intentions of suicide or murder, her outrageous hatred and her incredible laziness as well as her unstoppable mouth; and fourth, that his wife relinquished all rights and responsibilities to the child, the fruit of the marriage, never to see or communicate with her in any way, even via proxy; and fifth, that his wife knew that any violation of these agreements would result in forcing her husband to report her to the proper authorities for immediate incarceration on charges of violence, abuse, fraud, and mental anguish, among other causes, all documented and recorded; and sixth, that his wife was agreeing that no legal action against him or his family or his interests would ever be pursued by her or by her representatives at any time in the future; and lastly, that his wife had voluntarily ended her contract of agreement with him when she left the Quiet Recluse without his permission and her project work not then finished, and that in consideration of this and many other infractions the covenant of the marriage was thereby dissolved. And then, as he declared in court, he went over these terms with her for in the neighborhood of two hours, until she absolutely understood them he said, to which she then affixed her signature, accepting the $2000 he handed over. Then he drove her to Paducah where he put her on a bus bound for Batesville, Arkansas where a second cousin lived.

Within days Yvonne sent Tracy a post card pursuant to his request to have her address so that he could mail her belongings, and tacked on a plea asking for his consideration of allowing her to move back in the home with the family and her baby. He sent the belongings but rebuffed her plea. After two weeks passed she worked up enough courage to get in touch with her family in Fort Worth with whom there was a complete lacking of communication since her marriage in the spring of 1970.

Midway of October, with the assistance of her family, Yvonne did what Tracy couldn't have dreamed of in his wildest and when he eyed the paper work his mouth must have flown violently open. She filed for divorce, turning the tables against him with the firmest of conviction, citing irreconcilable differences, physical and mental cruelty, inappropriate martial conduct and contemporaneously filed a request for an emergency order granting her custody of the child, Connie Ann Delaney. In her affidavit supporting the request she explained the circumstances of the child's birth, depicted Tracy as a religious extremist, asserted that he and his mother controlled every aspect of her relationship with her daughter, and explicitly indicated they had denied contact with her in any form. And you guessed it Jacob; she attached the considerably damaging copies of the Provisions of Divorcement and Terms of Conditions Hereof and underscored that portion which purported to keep her from ever seeing her daughter again. Based on these and other representations in the affidavit the trial court issued a temporary restraining order against Tracy, and granted Yvonne custody of the child. Not long from that date, with the aid of the County Sheriff's Department, Yvonne went to the farm and retrieved Connie Ann Delaney from Tracy and the two of them were driven to Fort Worth by her attorney. At the time the mother had not seen her daughter since December, 1971. After she returned to Texas, Yvonne took Connie Ann to a pediatrician, the first physician to examine the child. He immediately started the immunization process."

Olga had joined us by now, coming over to sit on the other side of Mister Puryear, apologizing before taking a chair for her tardiness. She would only listen she explained, at least on the first, not yet ready to offer anything one way another. That would be her demeanor until close to when Mister Puryear finished. Likened to him she fore read the trial record multiple times, perhaps more than he.

"Looks like Tracy had neared the end of his road," I let out.

"It might look like it. But watch out. A tenacious guy, he would fight back as proved in his earlier exploits. In December, 1972 he filed a petition in the Kentucky trial court to set aside the previous order and decreed that Yvonne must return Connie Ann to him. He maintained that no defensible order existed in the first place sanctioning removal of the child from Kentucky and that no adequate proof could be supplied that irreparable harm would come to the child if she were restored to her father. With this order in hand he drove to Texas and with the help of the Fort Worth police regained custody of Connie Ann and brought her back to his Kentucky farm. But Yvonne proved that she could fight back too, for five days later she filed a motion for rights to visit with her child, at which time the trial court conducted a hearing on the matter, and on January 8 entered an order with which I wholly agree requiring both parties to undergo psychological evaluations. The mother's petition to visit her child was reset, the court stating that the hearing would be docketed for action after the psychological proceedings. A Doctor William Carney, PhD, drew the appointment to do the interviewing of the contestants. On January 12, 1973, Tracy filed his answer to Yvonne's petition for divorce as well as a counterclaim for divorce for himself. Up to his usual, he pointed up Yvonne's inappropriate martial conduct and claimed that she posed a danger to the child. In the meanwhile Doctor Carney in conjunction with Doctor Evelyn Wren, PhD, started the psychological evaluations of the parties. On January 16 and 17, 1973, the trial court Judge Ben Ellington presiding, there arose a hearing on the mother's petition for visitation. The mother, the father, and the mother in law testified with Doctor Carney and Doctor Wren speaking as to the mental stability of the mother and father. Doctor Carney noted problems with both parties but found in particular that Tracy lacked the emotional stability to raise the child, seemingly prone to lunging into excitement, and recommended that his visitations be supervised. Much of his recommendation rested on his belief that Tracy had demonstrated an inability to cooperate with Yvonne, and further recommended that he begin unsupervised visitations only after she believed he could cooperate with her. Doctor Carney also opined that so long as Tracy continued to attack Yvonne as unfit and incompetent for mothering it appeared unimaginable that he could give her the respect she deserved and needed as a primary caregiver. But then the other side of the coin surfaced. In contrast to Doctor Carney's position Doctor Wren opined that the mother would not be capable of parenting the child, while the father would be an effective parent. And what do you think about all this my young friend?" he asked, turning to me.

"Ha. It gets more intriguing by the minute. Aside from this, I'll offer that I'm not awfully surprised that the Doctors disagreed in their decisions and guess that Tracy at this juncture labored in a state of befuddled anxiety. "

"Yeah. Well, such is the way of divorce trials. They do get entangled and often turn in a bitter direction. You're not biased are you?" he asked in a tone of mirth. "Lawyer's are not supposed to become emotionally involved you know."

"You mean am I favoring the girl? I am, sort of. But I don't think it's biasness at work. I'm just honestly swayed by what I hear."

He killed a little time, in no manner hurried, seemingly immersed in something of depth while consulting his notes, then started again.

"I remember one place, where relevant to her appeal the mother testified that she likened her life with her husband to living in prison, going on from there that he and his mother wouldn't let her out of the house and that she had no freedom. And made references to locked doors, asserting that they locked her away from her daughter. She said that Tracy and his mother were able to cut her off from her parents by making her feel they were evil. Acting on these descriptions the trial court judge commented that 'It sounds like a cult,' and the mother added, 'I know it was.' The mother also denied Tracy's accusation that she screamed at him, contending that she only raised her voice. The mother's attorney referred to the farm in Kentucky as a 'two hundred fifty acre compound.' On January 21, relying on the psychological evaluations by Doctor Carney the trial court entered an order granting Yvonne temporary custody of Connie Ann and suspended the father's visitation pending the result of his evaluation not yet complete. The judge found the mother to be a credible witness and expressed his 'strong suspicion' that the father had caused her severe emotional trauma bordering on sinister. The father, urged on by his attorneys, then sought an interlocutory appeal from the judge's decision barring him from visiting his daughter, the appeal granted by the appellate court.

At this intermission some of the strangest unexpected things began to crop up. I was a bit confounded when I ran across them in the transcript of record. I wasn't in court when they came out. On the first I told you I wasn't there every minute."

"Yes sir. You did."

"Despite what the court alluded to as extreme allegations she had made about the father, Yvonne wrote letters to him on June 26, 1973 and July 7, 1973 attempting reconciliation, which must have caused her attorneys to lapse into fits. On July 21, 1973, the parties met at a park, both delighting at the progress of their daughter as she played and they talked, while the father stealthily recorded their conversation, in which Yvonne responded to his numerous pointed questions by admitting to him that during the marriage she broke her word over and over — the so called Promises — and conceded to him that her attorney had exaggerated some facts to the trial court in support of her petition for custody. In further response to Tracy's secretive interrogation Yvonne agreed that he had never put locks on her doors. She clarified that she assumed they were locked. She admitted too that they had reached a joint agreement not to invite her parents to their wedding and that she had spoken a falsity in her testimony that he alone disallowed an invitation to them. Further, she agreed that it was inaccurate to describe the farm as a compound or him as a cult leader in her court assertions. She also agreed that depicting him as the most controlling, dominant person in the universe amounted to a complete inaccuracy which she capped off by saying, 'Now that I see it, — Tracy doubtless helping her see it — it's wrong, but it lends itself to the exaggeration of how things were, when they really weren't that way.' Yvonne had to be more than shocked when learning that her secretly recorded admissions in the park were soon filed by Tracy in a first amended emergency motion to modify the order denying him visitation with the child. After receiving the motion Judge Ellington refused to hear proof, and in addition to this blow Tracy unknowingly teetered on the precipice of absorbing another. On September 13, 1973 Yvonne filed an affidavit in the trial court recanting the admissions she had made to her husband in the park, stating that she stood by her prior testimony in the case. She answered this way: 'I was only trying to reason with him to bring him back to truth and attempt to reconcile our marriage for the sake of our daughter who needed a father and for my sake, who needed a husband.' Judge Ellington again refused to hear the recordings. But as of September 28, 1973, in response to Doctor Carney's recommendation opted to permit the father to have supervised visitation with his daughter. But Tracy, ever emerging with the unexpected, perhaps smarting at the judge's decision not to listen to his secret recordings, on November 9, 1973 filed a separate lawsuit in the United States District Court for the Western District of Kentucky naming as defendants Judge Ellington,

Yvonne, her attorney, and Doctor Carney, boldly alleging among other things that Judge Ellington had made a false record of his divorce case and used his office as an offensive weapon. His complaint was summarily dismissed, the Federal court finding the father to be engaging in impertinent and scandalous allegations against the defendants and reminded him that the trial court had instructed him not to be speaking out with complaints of this nature. The defendants were consequently awarded their attorney's fees for defending the frivolous lawsuit, an amount totaling over $92,000, including $9,375 to the mother. All of which Tracy was compelled to pay."

"Wow! Tracy just wouldn't quit filing lawsuits. He needed to hire an attorney to tell him when to leave well enough alone."

"I think so. He had veered preposterously out of control and didn't seem to be aware before filing the petition the amount it might cost him. What he did, well; he acted most foolishly and in my opinion it worked against him in his other pursuits."

"Those against Yvonne?"

"Yes."

"Was that the last of the Federal court business?"

"Yes. To my knowledge. And just afterwards the trial court got going, though without Judge Ellington who removed himself from the case, and Doctor Carney no longer served on the case either, by his choice it might be presumed. The new judge for the trial court promptly ruled that Tracy posed no danger to Connie Ann, his daughter, and that he should be permitted to begin seeing her pending a final decision. The calendar page had turned. It was now January 4, 1974 and light could be seen at the end of the tunnel. The proceedings finally concluded on March 18, 1974. Testimonies were exhaustive, Tracy as vocal and vituperative as ever against his wife, while at the same time, prepped by her lawyers, she did not reflect shyness in facing up to him. The mother in law had testified too, but as expected in favor of her son, describing his relationship with his daughter as 'wonderful' and that when she stayed with them on the farm she and the father sang, played, collected eggs, and delighted at being around the cows, the horses, and the dogs. And further elaborated that Connie Ann didn't want to go back to the mother when her visitation time ended. To have seen them at large in the courtroom, Tracy and his mother, consorting with their attorneys especially between testimonial appearances, would have told you much more than I can here tell of their mind set, the internal whole of their demeanor, Tracy, sort of kinky headed boyish looking, grinning a counterfeit grin when hearing something to his favor from his lawyers; and his mother, a little old woman of sixty or past of not a strong physique exuding an air of proudness and conviction as she sat next to her son, which did not altogether vanish when she started to testify. There seemed to be a clever aura affixed to the lady that immovably caught my notice and I envisioned that this same cleverness, and guile, she had used during her son's youth to condition him much in the mold she had attempted to shape and control her daughter in law.

Then came the trial court decision, May 9, 1974.

In the memorandum of understanding the court noted that in the secret recordings of the meeting in the park the mother admitted to misstating certain facts by her exaggerations. But the greater significance in its view weighed upon the manner in which the parties interacted with one another. The finding contended that the father began when they met in the park to treat the mother as a child and for her part she immediately began to assume child like characteristics as she exchanged with her husband. The father's dominance clearly bled through. With respect to the designation of the primary residential parent an explanation was given that while perjury is a serious offense aimed at the integrity of the court the most important consideration had to be centered on the best interest of the child. The court allowed therefore that while the mother exaggerated some of the circumstances such did not affect the analysis concerning what had to be done. It did voice that the mother's misstatements would be dealt with in the awarding of attorneys fees, and then weighing all factors as a whole designated the mother as the primary residential parent of Connie Ann. I was there at the announcement. Tracy's face turned blood red and with eyes darting angrily looked over at his lawyers."

Olga spoke first. "I don't blame Yvonne a bit for her misstatements. I would have done the same thing if I'd been her. Look what she had to put up with. That guy was a rascal, a conniver, and did everything imaginable to do her in. The court had to see it."

"Vividly. Time and again," I threw in. "They particularily had to take a dim view of his secret recording trickery in the park."

Mister Puryear just looked at us and grinned, amused at his young lawyers.

"Now," he said. "This had to do with who got custody of the child. But the divorce! That's quite something else. So let us see.

Ample evidence appeared in the record to support the trial court's decision to award the divorce to the mother. Indeed, given the evidence, the trial court's findings regarding the father were charitable. Going into the marriage, they stressed, the mother obviously was immature, suggestible, and needy, while the father was controlling, dogmatic, and intolerant. 'These alone were daunting obstacles to overcome' they contended, 'but the active participation of the mother in law as a third prong doomed the marriage, setting up a dynamic in which she and her son combined first to indoctrinate the mother and then methodically humiliate, ostracize, and subjugate her.' The trial court rejected the father's assertion to the contrary, and found that he engaged in a egregious course of conduct which warranted a finding that he stood more at fault for the demise of the marriage. The preponderance of the evidence clearly supported the trial court's award of the divorce to the mother and the court announced that the decision was thereby affirmed."

The hour of three o'clock arrived and Mr. Puryear noticed. Folding his papers he pushed back from the table, not yet rising, nimbly placing his aging hands softly on his knees.

"That's it. What do you two have to say in the way of summary, or on anything that gnaws at you?"

It pleased me that Olga went first. It allowed me to better formulate my thoughts on something involving finances, always quite a significant thing when settling court suits is at issue.

"I read in the court records that the mother consented in spite of all that happened that she would willingly work with the father, Tracy, in his periods of visitation if she were given custody of the child, but in contrast the court pointed out that when the child stayed in the father's care he did not let the mother talk to her. This latter condition surely was a forceful consideration in bringing him down."

Mister Puryear nodded a slight. "That's a good way to put it." And then turned to me. "Jacob."

"The cost. Wow! So many lawyers, one petition filed after another, and the length of time before settlement. Did you have a look at the final sum?"

"As you indicate, the cost ran to a lofty amount, a total of $450,000 or more. Tracy disputed some of the discretionary costs allowed the mother for preparations by various specialists she'd hired for testimony. And some of these costs were lowered. One of the heavy whacks, an amount of $92,000 or thereabouts, resulted from the foolish decision of Tracy to bring suit against Judge Ellington and others in the Federal court. In the end Tracy was out a great bit of money and so too the mother, but far less, say $40,000, though someone else must have paid it for her, the parents likely, because she was broke. Her lawyers might have waived their fees. Sometimes they're pretty benevolent at doing things like that. The replacement for Judge Ellington in his traditional summary spoke that he hoped the both of them, husband and wife, learned a valuable lesson from the experience and that they would have acted wisely by settling their disputes outside the bounds of the court."

All three of us left after paying our bills, going back to the office where Mister Puryear took up a debt with a waiting client that someone failed to pay, while I, having stopped off at Olga's office, resumed discussion of the trial.

"What thoughts are uppermost with you in regard to the case?" I asked.

"Complicated, very; that's what stays with me more than anything else, besides my elation that Yvonne won. And also, Tracy's filing in the Federal court, an unexpected escapade, but on reflection of his character as described by Mister Puryear and the court trial records I can see why he was prone to do it. You'd have to agree that he's a headstrong rascal. Forbade one direction he was determined to excel in another, or at least he attempted to. But what are your thoughts?"

"That's easy. Mister Puryear said as he started telling me of the case that he'd witnessed the strangest marital dispute he ever ran across. I know that was so. I may practice law for fifty years though can't conceive that I'll ever encounter a conflict by any measure its equal. But there is something else that stirs me after I've had breathing room to put things in perspective."

"What's that?"

"It's about the child. The fierce harsh bitterness that the parents wrought on one another is a fact of the trial and I regret that things unfolded that way, particularly for Yvonne, but my sentiments reach out far more sympathetically to the child, the real victim. She deserved parents of a more stable stock. I find myself wishing that she has found life the smoothest of going in the years that have followed."